"Why are you l̶o̶o̶k̶i̶n̶g̶ we're a couple?"

Dax raked a hand over his cropped blond hair and blew out a sigh. Violet had only seen his authoritative sheriff side, but now here was the vulnerable, conflicted Dax. Both versions were much too intriguing, but she refused to get distracted. She'd only brought him some food to get him through the evening and morning of his moving day.

He didn't offer a response, which irked her even more. Those pretty eyes weren't going to get him out of this.

"I don't lie," she insisted.

His eyes snapped to hers. "I don't, either."

Vi quirked a brow. "That's a lie right there."

He stared at the ceiling for a brief moment before shifting his attention back to her.

"Listen, before five minutes ago, I've never lied to my family," he corrected. "But I need your help. They're only in town for two weeks. Can we pretend to get along in that amount of time? Ever since I moved here, they worry too much about me."

"Pretend to get along? You mean pretend to *date*?"

Julia Ruth is a *USA TODAY* bestselling author, married to her high school sweetheart and values her faith and family above all else. Julia and her husband have two teen girls and they enjoy their beach trips, where they can unwind and get back to basics. Since she grew up in a small rural community, Julia loves keeping her settings in fictitious towns that make her readers feel like they're home. You can find Julia on Instagram at juliaruthbooks.

Books by Julia Ruth

Love Inspired

Four Sisters Ranch

A Cowgirl's Homecoming
The Cowboy's Inheritance
The Sheriff Next Door

Visit the Author Profile page at LoveInspired.com.

THE SHERIFF NEXT DOOR

JULIA RUTH

LOVE INSPIRED
INSPIRATIONAL ROMANCE

LOVE INSPIRED®
INSPIRATIONAL ROMANCE

ISBN-13: 978-1-335-93191-7

Recycling programs for this product may not exist in your area.

The Sheriff Next Door

Love Inspired
22 Adelaide St. West, 41st Floor
Toronto, Ontario M5H 4E3, Canada
www.LoveInspired.com

Printed in Lithuania

MIX
Paper | Supporting responsible forestry
FSC® C021394

I have heard thy prayer, I have seen thy tears:
behold, I will heal thee.
—*2 Kings* 20:5

This book is dedicated to all of those people who deserve a second chance but might be afraid to take it. Have faith and trust God. Take that first step.

Chapter One

"Going on another blind date this weekend won't hurt, Vi. What else do you have to do?"

Violet Spencer pulled in a deep breath and prayed for patience with Jenn's well-meaning, yet displaced, meddling. Jenn Spencer, now Jenn Bennett, was just one of Violet's three siblings always trying to plan blind dates for her. But just because two of her sisters were now married didn't mean Vi wanted to be.

At one time, she'd thought she'd found the perfect partner, but Chance Parsons turned out to be manipulative and narcissistic. He'd completely obliterated her trust in men—and her own judgment.

"I'm really not interested," Violet insisted, like she always did.

"Well, it's already set up and Charles is supposed to text you," Jenn stated as if Vi hadn't objected.

"I'm almost to the clinic," she told her sister. "I'll have to talk to you later."

She said her goodbyes and disconnected the call as her favorite worship song pumped through her speakers. Another blind date was *not* happening. She'd been on three in the past month, like she was on some reality show, and she felt like she was starting to look desperate, which couldn't be further from the truth. It was her family that insisted she find someone to occupy her time. Her time was quite full without adding a man to the mix, thank you very much.

Running an animal clinic and working on the next adoption event for her rescues was rather taxing and time-consuming. Not to mention she hosted a small group ministry in her home once a week. She had what felt like a million things to do, so she'd have to figure out how to get out of this date. Not having a social life didn't mean she wasn't occupied with other things that filled her with joy.

Her annual pet adopt-a-thon, Pets in the Park, which she held through her clinic, usually filled her with joy. But this year, her right-hand man, Phil—who had always been so reliable and the perfect assistant for her event—had broken his leg and was laid up after emergency surgery. So here she was stuck doing everything. On top of that, her mind had been scattered lately between her parking violation from the new sheriff, the ministry group, and helping her family on the ranch. Right now she had so many balls in the air, she just had to pray they didn't all come bouncing down around her.

"And I will sing His praises!"

Violet belted out her favorite song as she approached the one and only stoplight in Rosewood Valley. She needed to relax and focus on anything other than the blind date she had to dodge and the mounting work looming ahead of her. She had to remain focused and avoid any and all distractions.

She glanced down to crank the tune up even more. Vi jerked her attention back up just in time to grip the wheel and see that the back of another car was much too close. She fumbled to brake, but her foot slipped. The impact of her car thudding into another jolted her body forward. Her airbag came out, smothering her face and making breathing difficult.

Though her car had come to an abrupt stop, the music continued to play as if nothing had happened.

Violet shoved the airbag out of her face and pulled in a deep breath, trying to assess her body all at once. She didn't think she was hurt and she hoped the people in the car in front of her were okay, too. She'd never been in an accident in her life.

With a shaky hand, Violet opened her car door

and stepped out. Her heart beat way too fast and she really didn't know what to do, but the moment she turned her attention to the vehicle, she groaned.

Great. Just what she didn't need. She'd rear-ended a deputy. When the driver stepped out, she fully expected to see Wyatt or Ben, but no. This was a stranger and not one of the guys she'd gone to high school with—which meant only one thing.

This was the new sheriff.

Nothing like a forced meeting with the town's latest resident. Tall, almost imposingly so with that dark uniform. His light hair peeked from beneath his black Stetson, and he had a smooth, chiseled jawline that had her heart beating faster now for an entirely different reason. Why didn't anyone warn her that he was so handsome?

"Are you alright?" she called to him as he moved toward her. The stranger was a good foot taller than her and that cowboy hat only made him seem even more commanding.

He removed his sunglasses and held her in place with vibrant blue eyes. A definite surprise. She wasn't sure what she'd been expecting from the new sheriff—maybe someone older with a thicker midsection and a disapproving scowl. Not a handsome, striking thirtysomething who made every logical thought vanish and who had her stomach in knots.

She'd been deceived by a good-looking man before. Never again.

"I'm fine," he replied.

His low smooth tone caught her off guard, but she wasn't looking for attraction or anything else. At this point, she certainly wasn't looking for another ticket, either, but she doubted she'd be able to dodge that considering his brake light now dangled onto his bumper and was held in place by only a wire. Oops. One of these days, her insurance was just going to drop her.

"Are you hurt?" he asked, taking a step forward.

Violet shook her head. "No. Just shaky."

"Were you texting and driving?" he asked, furrowing his brows.

"Texting? What? No, of course not," she insisted. "I've never done that. My foot slipped on the brake when I turned up my music."

The sheriff propped his hands on his hips and blew out a sigh, then muttered something she couldn't understand.

"Excuse me?" she asked.

He shook his head. "We need to move the cars over to let traffic through and then I'll get a report going... What's your name?"

Violet glanced around and waved as a nosy

driver crept by them to get through the light. "Violet… Spencer."

He nodded, as if the name appeared familiar. *Great.* "Can you drive your car?" he asked.

"I believe so."

"Don't hit anything else."

With that snippy parting shot, he slid back into his cruiser and moved over to the side of the road.

Well, this first impression wasn't going well. She might as well go ahead and text her office assistant that she'd be late meeting the guy helping her with her rental equipment for the adopt-a-thon. She had a feeling Sheriff Adams wasn't in the mood for all the reasons she needed to hurry up and get this over with.

Dax Adams focused on remaining calm. Distracted driving was the one thing he absolutely would not tolerate. He didn't care the reasoning, radio or texting. People's lives could be changed in an instant… He should know.

Once his dented cruiser was safely out of the way and in a side lot, he got back out and waited on Violet Spencer to join him. He hadn't met the local veterinarian in person before now, but he'd heard she wasn't too happy with the parking violation he'd left her with a while back. He'd met with her sister Rachel and had discussions about the upcoming town council fundraiser that was to be held on their farm, Four Sisters. But this was his first encounter with Violet.

Still, he wasn't in town to make friends. He was in town to start a new life and be the best public servant he knew how to be. At this stage in his life, he had to thrust himself fully into this new chapter and keep moving forward. Alone.

As Violet pulled in behind him, he assessed the damage to her front end. Drivable, but her airbag had deployed and her front end was a bit rough. She'd be finding another mode of transportation for the foreseeable future—as would he.

"I'm really so sorry," she started as she adjusted the knot of hair on top of her head. "Is there any way to speed this process along or maybe do it later? I'm due at the clinic to meet this guy who rents tents for my event and—"

"We will do this now."

He cut off her rambling because he honestly didn't care why she couldn't make time for this. She should have thought about that before she decided to fiddle with her radio, if that's what she'd actually been doing.

"Will this take long?" she asked, pulling her cell from the pocket of her green scrub top. "I need to let my assistant know when I'll be there."

Dax tried to ignore the fact that her green

uniform matched her eyes or the fact that green was his favorite color. He shouldn't be intrigued by her natural beauty, especially when he was agitated, but he couldn't help how he felt. The unwanted, instant attraction threw him off, and honestly, made him a tad cranky.

"This would go a lot faster if you'd put your phone away and get your insurance information, license and registration for me to start this report."

Her eyes darted from her phone to him as her lips thinned. Well, join the crowd. He was none too happy, either.

To his surprise, she didn't have a snappy comeback or another excuse. She merely nodded and went back to her car to retrieve the necessary items. He had reasons to get home as well, but none of that mattered right now. The company delivering the last of his furniture would have to wait or leave things on the porch. He couldn't be in two places at once.

Times like this, he wished he had his family close to call on for support, but he'd had to move. Staying in Oregon with so many memories and potentially being smothered by his loving, well-meaning family wouldn't have been good for him in the long run. Dax fully believed coming to Rosewood Valley was God opening a door that Dax needed to walk through. So he did. This move would be good for him and he'd already settled nicely into his role and was getting along with the deputies. He'd instantly felt welcome at the post.

"Have a seat in the cruiser." He gestured toward the back seat as he took the documents from her. "This will be a few minutes. There's protocols and an order so there's no rushing the process."

Without waiting for her to answer, he slid back into his cruiser, ready to get this done and get home. He'd gone in this morning to talk to the midnight deputies and hadn't planned on being gone this long, but here he was, now running late to meet with the movers bringing his things to his new home.

The moment that Violet settled into the car, Dax realized he'd made a mistake. Some floral aroma wafted around him and thrust him back to another time, and another woman with the same floral fragrance. He'd know that scent anywhere—he'd purchased it for many birthdays.

Pulling in a deep breath and attempting to focus on the job at hand, Dax started putting all of the pertinent information into his computer.

"I'm not a bad driver," she stated after a long yawn of silence. "I mean, I had that parking violation, but I'd parked there for years and nobody said anything."

Dax grunted as he typed in her birthday. Three years younger than him. She looked to be about ten years younger, or maybe he'd just aged more than he thought since becoming a widower.

"I'm not sure why that was a problem," she went on.

Dax stopped typing and cast a glance her way. "Because you were parked in a 'no parking' zone. I can't help that the rules weren't enforced before I arrived, but now you know so I'm not sure why we need to discuss it."

"Because I feel I wasn't in the wrong," she retorted.

"Feelings aren't taken into consideration when breaking the law."

Despite her huff of silent disagreement, Dax went back to the report. This would take a little extra time considering this accident wasn't typical. The sheriff's vehicle wasn't usually the one in the accident.

"You don't have a very good opinion of me." She didn't ask; she stated.

"I frankly haven't thought about my opinion of you," he replied without looking back. He was trying to avoid too much eye contact considering her perfume still enveloped him like a familiar friend. "I've been a little busy since getting to town." He'd been staying at a B and

B until closing the deal on his new house—and today was moving day.

As he put in more information, Violet pulled out her cell and seemed to be firing off texts. He could appreciate the fact she had things to do—so did he. He wasn't too thrilled about this situation, either.

"You've got to be kidding me," she muttered. *Don't ask. Don't ask.* "Is there a problem?"

He couldn't help himself and the question just popped out.

She blew out a sigh and dropped her phone to her lap. "Just a disastrous blind date in the making."

The idea of a blind date sounded absolutely revolting, but thankfully he never had that problem. "Not a fan?"

He'd been on a couple dates since his wife passed, but they'd been with friends and he wouldn't classify them as anything even remotely romantic. He wasn't sure he'd ever be ready for that again.

She sighed. "One of my sisters thinks she's found me the perfect guy."

"And you don't believe her?"

Why did he keep asking questions? They both had things to do and this getting-to-know-you portion of the day wasn't on the list.

"First, nobody is perfect," she stated. "Second,

I don't have time for dating, blind or otherwise. But since she recently married, she wants to play Cupid and I feel like a jerk for telling her no."

A meddling family? While Dax might be annoyed at her terrible driving sense, he did feel sympathy. His own family could be a bit overwhelming at times, though he never doubted their love for him.

If Violet's sister was trying to set her up on a blind date, why was she so resistant? Did she not believe in love or did she just enjoy being single?

When she muttered back down at her phone, he collected his thoughts. Finishing this report was all he needed to do. Not worry about this adorable veterinarian's social life. He needed to keep his own life on track and moving forward. There was no time to get distracted by a set of pretty green eyes.

He'd been in love once. Losing his soulmate had been the worst experience of his life. He never wanted to go through that type of pain again.

Chapter Two

Dax stared at the stacks of boxes and the lack of furniture in his new home. The overwhelming desire to run away started to consume him, but this move was good. He needed this change, even if the idea terrified him.

Being a widower at the age of thirty-three was never something he thought would happen to him. It had been three years without June, and Dax knew his late wife would want him to move on. The only way he knew to do that was to start fresh somewhere else, away from the memories they'd made together in their hometown. So when the sheriff position opened in Rosewood Valley, he took that as a sign from God.

Dax's great-great-grandfather had been the first sheriff in this town over one hundred years ago, so Dax felt it fitting he come here. The move from Oregon to Northern California wasn't too hard, and getting to know a brand-new town and its residents would be good to keep his mind focused.

Granted getting rear-ended earlier by the agitated yet striking Violet Spencer when her "foot slipped" hadn't been in his plans. Distracted driving had ruined his life once already, so he'd probably come across as a bit gruff. Still, he took his job seriously—especially now.

He'd never moved into a new home alone like this. When he'd gotten married at the age of nineteen, he'd moved into his first apartment with June. Then they moved a few years later into what he thought would be their forever home.

God had different plans and there wasn't a doubt in Dax's mind that God's hand was on this move as well. So long as Dax continued down the path laid out before him, he'd be okay. He had faith and that's what had gotten him through these past few years.

Dax figured he'd get some boxes unpacked and then head into town for dinner. He'd started his new job a couple months ago, but he'd been staying in a cozy B and B until he'd found the right home. Thanks to a local Realtor whom he could now call a friend, Dax was ready to set roots in the town that had helped water the roots of his ancestors.

Dax made his way toward the back of the house, deciding to start in the kitchen. He'd throw the dishes and pantry items in the cabinets and call it a day in there. If he could do one room per day, he'd feel a little more settled within the week. It wasn't like he had a ton of items anyway. He'd purged quite a bit before the move so he didn't have to pack it all, and there were just some items he'd been holding on to since Junie's passing that it was time to let go of. Dax was fully ready to embrace this fresh start.

A two-bedroom, two-bath home would be more than spacious enough for him. He could make his new memories here and not be haunted by the empty rooms. Transitions were difficult, but Dax planned to make this a positive time in his life and look for all the good he could find.

He'd just tossed the last empty box by the back door when the sounds of the doorbell echoed through the house. His first guest? Maybe Jack Hart, his Realtor, coming to check in.

Dax maneuvered down the narrow hallway, made even more narrow by the boxes lining it. Through the etched glass of the old oak door, he spotted someone quite familiar. Pulling in a deep breath, he closed the distance to the door and flicked the lock, then turned the knob beneath his palm.

Apparently she was just as surprised about who she found on the other side of the door, if her wide eyes and O-shaped mouth were any indication.

"You're my new neighbor?" she asked.

Neighbor...? Of course this woman would be his neighbor. Why not? Apparently God wanted to truly put Dax up to a challenge of relying on his faith with this new move.

Dax glanced out the door and scanned the open space. Homes weren't directly next to each other like where he'd come from, and he appreciated the distance.

"If you live to the right or left of me, I guess I am," he replied, bringing his focus back to her and the foil-wrapped package in her hand. "Does that mean you're taking your neighborly gift back?"

Her lips twitched as if suppressing a smile and he found that he wanted to see her smile, which was absurd. He should be unpacking boxes, not unpacking the charming looks of his neighbor.

"My mother raised me better than that," she volleyed back. "Homemade banana bread. It's still warm."

His mouth watered at the mere idea of warm, homemade bread. Taking a step back, he motioned her inside. "Come on in." Because his mother also raised him right.

Her wide green eyes met his a moment before she nodded and stepped over the threshold.

"I can't stay long," Violet stated as she extended the loaf. "And I'm sure you have plenty to do as well."

Clearly she needed an excuse or an outlet so she could go when she wanted. That was fine. The fact she didn't snatch her bread and go back to her side of the property line was shocking.

The sweet aroma from the baked good wafted all around him and he couldn't help but ask, "When did you have time to make bread after we parted ways?" It had been several hours, but still.

She shrugged as she crossed her arms. She'd changed out of her scrubs and into a pair of jeans and a short-sleeved pink T-shirt. With her hair in a ponytail, she had that wholesome girl-next-door vibe, unlike the flustered driver who had rear-ended him. Unfortunately for him, both versions of Violet Spencer were cute.

"I've been home a few hours," she explained. "I saw the moving van and wondered who had moved in. I could've asked my brother-in-law but decided to just come see for myself."

"Your brother-in-law?"

"Jack Hart," she added. "He married my sister Rachel."

Dax had heard of the Spencer sisters through Jack, but he hadn't met any of the other sisters yet. He'd been so preoccupied with trying to get to know the town and the laid-back way of life here, he was still learning the locals.

"Why don't we share this." The offer spilled out before he could think twice, but he wasn't about to be rude, especially when they'd both had a taxing day. "I can't eat the entire loaf myself."

Before she could answer, a vibrating sound emanated from her back pocket. She pulled out her cell phone and groaned.

"Another blind date?" he asked.

Violet nodded as her fingers flew over the screen. "I know my sisters love me, but I don't have time to date, nor am I ready to walk down the aisle. Why does everyone think that because I'm single I just want to throw on a white dress and head to the altar?"

She pocketed her cell once again and shifted her focus back to him. "I'm thrilled for them, but marriage or even a relationship isn't a priority for me just yet."

Marriage had been absolutely everything to him, but there was no way he wanted to jump back into anything serious. Right now, he needed to take it one day at a time and get used to this move and this new chapter. It had taken time to get used to waking up alone and eating at a table for two with only one plate. Buying groceries for one had been an adjustment as well. Nobody had prepared him for all of the changes—they'd only told him about the heartache.

"My family loves me, but the meddling is getting a bit out of control," she went on with a groan. "I don't know how to let them down nicely when they only have my best interest at heart."

Dax motioned for her to follow him down the hallway toward the kitchen. "I get it," he agreed. "That's one of the reasons I moved here. I needed a little bit of space from my family. They definitely love me, but at times they can be a bit much, especially since I lost my wife."

Violet's soft gasp gave him pause. Of course she wouldn't know his backstory.

Dax cringed as they stepped into the kitchen, then turned to face her. "I didn't say that for pity. I'm just explaining my situation."

Violet's eyes didn't hold pity, and when he looked at her he saw something akin to understanding and sincerity. Maybe they had gotten off on the wrong foot or perhaps she just didn't like him initially. Perhaps she'd suffered her own pain. He had no clue, but they did share the common bond that they had interfering families and no interest in dating.

"Then I'll offer my condolences," she stated. "While I've never lost someone that close to me, my sister lost her husband several years back. A loss that deep definitely reshapes your life."

"I think mine is still reforming," he muttered.

Violet let out a soft sigh and glanced around. "So, where are your knives? And do you put butter or cream cheese on your bread?"

Thankfully, she didn't dissect him about his feelings and emotional wounds. He actually found himself smiling at her abrupt turnaround to the food.

"With warm, homemade bread, I don't put anything on it," he replied. "And I haven't gotten to the grocery yet, so…"

"No worries. I prefer it just the way it is as well."

She took the bread back from him, went to the counter and started digging through drawers he'd filled just this evening. He started to tell her where the silverware was, but she found it all on her own. She started humming and something clenched at his heart. Granted this home was brand-new to him so he hadn't made any memories, but it had still been quite some time since a woman made herself at home in his kitchen. And the humming… He recognized that familiar song because his twin sister often sang it in church.

"So how many blind dates have you been set up on?" he asked, staying on a safe topic and dodging all talk of parking tickets or accident reports and late wives.

Violet tore off two paper towels from the random roll sitting on the counter and placed two evenly sliced pieces of bread on each one. When she crossed back to him and handed him his slice, he tried to avoid touching her hand at all costs. He failed. That tingle of awareness couldn't be ignored, but he also couldn't dwell on this moment, either. His mind was just confused and flustered by an attractive woman who'd done something thoughtful. Probably had she known he was the one over here, she would've burnt the bread before dropping it off and leaving.

"Too many," she answered around a bite of the snack. "I take that back. Probably just a handful, but that's too many in my opinion. I've got so much going on with my clinic and no-kill animal shelter. Aside from the fact I'm the only small animal vet in the county, my annual fundraiser and animal adoption event is coming up and my right-hand man is down after he broke his leg and had surgery."

Dax listened as he finished the most amazing bread he'd ever had. Maybe he could eat this entire loaf after all. He wondered if he could pay her to make more on a routine basis or if that would sound too desperate.

"I'm sorry." She swallowed. "I'm rambling and I really didn't come to dump my issues onto my new neighbor." She wiped her hands with her napkin and glanced around for the trash. "I'll just clean up and let you get back to unpacking. Or whatever else you need to do."

She tossed her trash into the can by the back door and went over to the counter to wrap the bread back in the foil. There was a bold confidence about her that intrigued him. So perhaps it was best she was leaving. He didn't need any distractions, and Violet Spencer was seriously starting to become just that.

When she turned back to face him, she tipped her chin and leveled a gaze with those emerald eyes. "I really am sorry about earlier. You're going to think I just disobey the law and do whatever I want."

"The idea might have entered my mind," he admitted.

Violet crossed her arms. "I was raised to respect authority. I'll take full blame for the accident."

"And the parking ticket?"

She lifted one slender shoulder. "Considering I parked there for years, I think a ticket was a bit harsh."

"We can agree to disagree," he replied, offering a smile.

"I imagine we will disagree on more than this." She chuckled as she made her way toward the foyer. "If you need anything, I'm just on the other side of that field." She stepped through the doorway.

"Thanks for the bread."

Without turning around, she merely threw up a hand and waved.

Dax watched as she left and wondered how this woman had gone from slamming into his cruiser to baking for him in the span of just a day. One thing was for sure, he had a feeling this was not his last run-in with the adorable, yet frustrating, Violet Spencer.

Violet scolded herself as she headed back toward town in the car she'd thankfully been able to borrow from her mother. She had a million and one things to do yet she found herself running an impromptu errand for her new neighbor a mere hour since she'd last seen him.

And why? She kept asking herself that very question. He'd irritated her about not seeing her perspective with the parking violation. Yet here she was being a faithful servant. She told herself she was doing this service to be the hands and feet of God, but there was that small part of her that couldn't deny Dax's good looks and charm might have something to do with it.

And when he'd discussed his late wife, something had churned in her heart. She wouldn't give him the pity he'd clearly had enough of, but she also wouldn't be rude—so long as she didn't get any more tickets.

Another handsome man from another time filled her mind and reminded her of why she vowed to remain single for a good while. She believed there were good men in this world— her father and her two brothers-in-law to name a few—but she couldn't trust her judgment. Not after Chance had left her with a broken heart and a series of doubts. The betrayal of finding he'd been lying to her about everything made trusting difficult.

Throwing herself into her clinic and no-kill animal shelter had gotten her through some tough times. Her animals never lied to her and they loved her unconditionally. That was all she needed for now.

As Violet turned off the two-lane country road and onto the main street taking her into town, her cell rang. She tapped the hands-free button on her steering wheel to answer.

"This is Violet."

"Violet, this is Vernon."

She cringed as her grip tightened. "Yes. I'm so sorry I couldn't make our appointment earlier. There was a slight emergency." They were supposed to meet to finalize equipment rentals for her event.

"I heard," he replied. "Nothing to apologize

for. I just want to touch base with a few of the things that need your immediate attention. Phil used to handle this, but with him out of commission, you'll have to tell me what you'd like."

As he rattled off a list of all the rental equipment they'd used in the past, like tents and food trucks, her mind started spinning. This was why she had Phil. He focused on the logistics like that while she concentrated on the animals and finding them good homes at the event. But she could do this on her own or incorporate the help of one of her sisters, though they were just as busy as she was.

"Since this is not in my wheelhouse, would it be best to go off what we did last year?" she asked.

"We absolutely can, but I do recall Phil stating that he thought we didn't have enough tables and play yard areas for the puppy section and potential families looking to adopt. Should I ask him?"

Violet made another turn into the parking lot of the grocery store. "No, no. I don't want to bother him when he's laid up. Let me get to my computer and double-check last year's numbers and I'll text you later tonight. Is that okay?"

"Absolutely fine. No rush. I have nothing else booked that day, so you're good."

"Okay. I'll get back with you this evening," she assured him. "Thanks so much."

Once she disconnected the call and pulled into a parking spot, the first fat drop of rain hit the windshield. Well, she might as well get in, get the necessities and get out. She couldn't let a little pop-up storm stop her and she fully intended to prove to the new sheriff that she wasn't some flighty rule-breaker. She wanted to live in peace, especially with her new neighbor. And she could start by extending this olive branch.

She'd just have to keep her mind and eyes on what was important right now, and that was keeping all these balls up in the air all while learning how to juggle. No problem.

Chapter Three

Feeling quite proud of his accomplishment and very much worn-out, Dax grabbed a cold glass of ice water and surveyed his living room. He'd finished the majority of the kitchen just before Violet had showed. After she'd left, he had a new burst of energy and went to unpack some of the books into the built-ins on either side of the original redbrick fireplace. He preferred the original charm to any painted facade.

This whole house reminded him of something June would've loved. Perhaps leaving all of their memories behind in Oregon was for the best, but she would never fully leave him. And he liked to think she was proud of this step he'd taken to heal his heart. He also realized that he could think about her now without breaking down and thinking he couldn't go on, thanks to a great support system and years of therapy. He'd packed photos of her and brought them with him and placed one on the dresser in his bedroom. He'd thought about putting framed images all over, but then remembered he needed to take this move slow. If he had her in every room of the house, he might not be able to fully move on and make those new memories.

Just as he started to kick back in his new leather recliner, his doorbell rang.

Violet again? Maybe with more bread because he had a feeling that loaf she'd brought earlier would be gone by morning.

He stepped through the wide, arched doorway and turned in the foyer but stilled.

Three very familiar faces stared back at him through the glass in the door. What on earth were they doing here?

Something between a sigh and a laugh escaped him as he closed the distance and turned the lock. Swinging the door wide, he offered a wide smile to the most important people in his life. His family.

"You guys aren't seriously standing on my porch."

"Surprise," his twin sister exclaimed as she held out her arms to pull him into an embrace.

Dax fell into Clara's warm hug and patted her back. He shouldn't be shocked at their unannounced visit, yet he was. They'd all been so worried when he'd told them he was moving so far away. He had no family, no friends, absolutely nothing in this new town except a job, the history of his great-great-grandfather and prospects of a new life.

"You guys could've texted or called," he stated, pulling back to hug his mother and father. "I don't even have my own bedsheets on, let alone the guest bedroom made up."

"Oh, we booked that cute little bed-and-breakfast down the road," his mother informed him. The one he'd been staying in the past few months. They knew it was moving day, and they'd clearly timed their surprise visit to help. She kissed his cheek and patted the other one as her smile spread across her face. "You look so good. We missed you but wanted to give you some space to get settled into town before we bombarded you."

He hadn't seen them since he'd left Oregon, other than video calls. His entire life he'd lived in the same town as his sister and parents, so not having them within a few miles had seemed weird, and he wasn't too proud or masculine to admit it was great having them show up. Though he wasn't quite set up for guests yet.

He shouldn't be surprised they'd shown today to help. It was just who they were. Giving him the space to find his footing but showing up when he needed them most.

"Come on in." He stepped aside so they could

enter. "Watch all the boxes. Or better yet, grab one and lend a hand."

"I told your mother we should let you get settled," his father explained. "But you know once she gets something in her head, there's no talking her out of it, and she knew the movers were coming today."

Dax followed them in and closed the door behind him. "Don't worry about it. They got my living room furniture, kitchen table and two beds in place. I've done a few things today but just called it quits so there's still plenty to unpack."

"We're here for the next two weeks." His sister beamed. "We can help with anything you need."

Two weeks? Dax wondered what was up if they planned on such a lengthy stay.

"How can you take off work that long?" he asked his sister. She had a very demanding job as a maternity ward nurse.

Clara shrugged. "I never take time off and had enough vacation built up. Besides, there are other nurses to help deliver babies. I wanted to come see my little brother's new place."

"You're only older by eight minutes," he reminded her, just like he always did when she brought up their age difference like she was superior.

She winked and offered that signature grin that looked so much like his. "I'm still in charge."

As she walked through the wide opening leading to the living room, she did a big circle and gave a slow nod. "Such great potential with the right paint and artwork. This fireplace is stunning with the detail work on the mantel."

"Be careful or she'll have the entire place painted by morning," his father murmured.

"I can hear you, you know," Clara replied, still staring at the fireplace.

Dax chuckled as he eased around a tower of totes to step into the living room. "I'm fine with the paint colors as they are," he informed his sister.

She gasped as she turned to him. "Gray? Everyone does gray. Why don't you liven this room up with a pale yellow or sage green? Oh, a royal blue would be masculine yet still cozy with the whole cottage vibe."

His wife always wanted colored walls and he'd turned over total decorating control to her to make their house how she wanted. He just couldn't do all the colors again, not if he wanted to start living his own life. Each decision he made had to be a little selfish now so he could continue on his healing journey. While he missed June and cherished the life they'd made, she would want him to move on and find peace and joy once again.

"I think I'll just work on unpacking and settling into a new job and my new town for now."

"And how's that going?" his mother asked, stepping up beside him and placing her hand on his arm. "The job? Do you like it?"

"It's going pretty well, minus the fender bender I was in this morning in my patrol car."

His mom jerked back, and her eyes widened as she asked, "Were you hurt?"

He shrugged. "Just annoyed."

And he still wasn't sure if he was more annoyed at the actual accident or the fact a certain beautiful woman wouldn't get out of his mind. Oh, she'd been fired up and agitated, but so had he. Then she'd popped in and they'd shared a normal moment over warm bread and he saw her from a totally different side. Something about her seemed familiar, yet fresh and exciting. He didn't recall the last time a woman had his thoughts in a tangle of knots.

He almost couldn't wait to see where their next encounter took them. She'd keep him on his toes—that was for certain—and he didn't know if he should be concerned or…

"Honey, are you alright?"

His mother's question pulled him from the mixed feelings rolling through him. He shouldn't be attracted to someone. That didn't seem right…did it? He knew June would want him to move on, but moving on in a town and career were one thing. Moving on with a woman was something entirely different.

"Of course," he assured her with a smile. "Why wouldn't I be?"

"They're afraid you're running." His dad's voice seemed to boom the bold statement as he pointed between Dax's mother and sister.

"Running?" he repeated. "Maybe toward a new life, but not away from my past. I carry those memories with me every single day."

"We're just worried you're here all alone and coming home to an empty house would be depressing," his sister explained.

"I went home to an empty house for the past three years," he reminded her. "I can't keep living in a place that reminds me of all I lost."

His mother gave his arm another gentle squeeze before releasing him. "We can't help but worry, Dax. This is such a drastic move with no one to help you."

"I have help," he explained. "I've made a few friends."

His Realtor, Jack, and the deputies had all welcomed him in like family.

Besides, Dax wasn't one to throw a party or anything. He didn't need to have gatherings to get settled in. He was a single guy. He didn't do things like that. Actually, he'd been seriously considering getting a dog. Now that he was out of the B and B, it'd be the perfect way to fill his new home and make some new memories.

"We want you to move on and be happy," Clara added. "We're just here to make sure that happens. Maybe there's a nice single woman in town—"

"Clara," he started, but was cut off by the doorbell.

Not that he was upset about the interruption. Clara had been asking him about a woman since he moved and he'd dodged the questions and ignored the photos she'd sent of nearby singles she'd found online. She'd gone so far as to ask if she could make him a profile on a dating app. No, thanks. If God had a woman for him, He would put her right in Dax's path so there was no confusion.

Dax turned the knob and swung the door wide, shocked to see Violet Spencer once again on his doorstep. He'd been so distracted by his thoughts, he hadn't looked through the glass to see who was there. No wrapped loaf this time, but Violet held an armful of grocery bags.

He immediately reached for them. "What is all this?" he asked.

"You didn't have food," she explained. "You need something to get you going and you can't live on banana bread alone."

After the way they'd left things she was now showing up with groceries? Had she taken pity on him?

Before he could thank her for the food, or reply in any manner, his sister's voice sounded from right behind him.

"Oh, who do we have here?" she asked, reaching beyond Dax to extend her hand. "I'm Dax's twin sister, Clara."

Violet's smile spread across her face. "I'm Violet," she replied, shaking his sister's hand. "I just wanted to bring some groceries since his kitchen is bare. Well, except for the bread I brought earlier."

"Oh, she bakes, too?" Clara gave him a waggle of her brows. "I had no idea my brother had found someone so beautiful and talented. Come on in."

Dax stared at Violet as her bright green eyes darted between him and Clara. "She can come back later," he stated, trying to save them both.

"What? Nonsense." Clara completely steamrollered over his words. "Our parents would love to meet your girlfriend."

"I'm not—" Violet started.

"Girlfriend?" His mother's squeal of a question echoed behind him and cut off Violet's defense. Dax, for his part, stood there frozen, unable to find the words to explain.

"Welcome," his mother greeted as she tried to wedge herself in the doorway as well.

The gesture pushed Dax out onto the porch next to Violet.

"Please, come in." His mom gestured her into the house. "We just got here. This is perfect timing."

"But I'm—"

"She's not—" He and Violet spoke at the same time.

"A girlfriend?" His father stepped into the conversation and reached out to pull Violet into an embrace.

"This is just wonderful," his dad stated as he hugged Violet. "Here we were, worried how Dax was settling, but clearly he's doing well. Now, come on in and let's talk."

Violet was hustled inside, but she tossed a glance over her shoulder and all he could do was clutch the grocery bags and wonder how in the world he'd lost control of this situation.

And to think she just wanted to do a nice gesture for her new neighbor? Now Violet found herself in a "relationship" and meeting the family. This had certainly escalated quickly.

She almost laughed at the misunderstanding. She could see how bringing Dax groceries and the mention of baking for him could've suggested a closeness between them that wasn't really there, and Dax was clearly just as confounded as she was. He'd set his family straight—once he finished pouting on the porch. She'd never been a fan of deceit or lying and she wasn't about to partake in those activities now.

But she'd let Dax take charge because this was his family. Maybe she should feign some excuse to get back home. She still had to give meds to her foster pups, so there was that.

"I didn't catch your name, dear," Dax's mother said.

Violet stood in the living room amidst one boring brown recliner and stacks of boxes labeled "Books" and "Pictures." She assumed them to be empty since the shelves seemed full.

She found three sets of eyes on her, but she felt the presence of Dax behind her. Much too close, yet somehow reassuring. Odd she even had that feeling, but considering he was the only one here she somewhat knew, she had to cling to that.

"I'm Violet," she answered. "I live next door."

"Oh, is that how you two met?" his sister asked.

Vi turned her attention to Dax's twin and easily saw the resemblance. They were clearly siblings, but no doubt the twin vibe was strong. Same crisp blue eyes, light hair, soft smile. Even though they'd just met in person this morning, she had only seen him smile a couple of times. Mostly all she'd seen was a haunting behind his eyes and something else she couldn't quite identify. He had a cloud of mystery that surrounded him, or maybe that was a wall of defense, she wasn't quite sure. But having lost his wife made the enigma surrounding him make a little more sense.

"We met through work," Dax offered, coming to stand beside her as if in support.

Vi continued to bite her tongue, waiting for him to explain she'd rear-ended him and they were barely friends, let alone dating.

"That's wonderful," his sister added. Her eyes darted to Violet. "You're just so pretty and sweet for bringing bread and groceries. My brother can't cook or bake so hopefully you'll help him there. He gets into his work and doesn't always take care of himself."

"I'm not a toddler," he defended. "I can grab takeout as easy as anyone else."

Vi opened her mouth to clear up the misunderstanding and make a quick exit when—

"Junk," Clara corrected. "You mean you eat junk."

"She's not wrong," his mother chimed in. "Maybe you should take some cooking classes."

"In what spare time?" his father asked.

As the family went around and around on how

Dax needed a "keeper," Violet took a slow step backward, then another.

Dax caught her gaze. "We're just going to put those bags in the kitchen…" He held her stare. "Would you help me for a minute?"

She nodded while he picked up the bags. "Excuse us," he told his family.

Dax led the way toward the back of the house and into the kitchen. She waited until he set the sacks on the small round table before she demanded an explanation.

"What is going on?" she whispered through gritted teeth. "Why are you letting them believe we're a couple?"

Dax raked a hand over wavy blond hair and blew out a sigh as he leaned against the counter. She'd only seen the authoritative side, but now here was the vulnerable, conflicted Dax. Both versions were much too intriguing, but she refused to get distracted. She'd only brought some food to get him through the evening and morning. She hadn't wanted to come in again and get even more acquainted.

Silence settled heavy between them as chatter from the front room filtered down the hallway. He didn't offer a response, which irked her even more. Those pretty blue eyes weren't going to get him out of this.

"I don't lie," she insisted.

His eyes snapped to hers. "I don't, either."

Vi quirked a brow. "That's a lie right there."

He let out a low groan and stared at the ceiling for a moment before shifting his attention back to her.

"Listen, before five minutes ago I've never lied to my family," he corrected. "But I need your help. You've seen what they're like. They're only in town for two weeks. Can we pretend to get along in that amount of time? They worry so much and I'm just trying to give them some peace about my drastic move."

Shocked at his request, Violet took a step back. Then she pulled a chair out and sank down. "Pretend to get along? You mean pretend to date?"

He nodded slowly. "I guess that's what we'd call it."

When she said nothing, he pushed off the counter and crossed to her. He pulled out the other chair and flipped it around to straddle it. He sat much too close and she could see the variety of blues in those sad eyes. Her heart started to ache for the pain in him that she didn't even understand, but she had to focus on her own issues.

"I would never ask this of you if I didn't think this was the best way to make them believe that I truly am okay with this move," he added softly. "We don't even have to go on a real date. Just pop over every now and then and act like you like me."

She shook her head. "I can't lie to people, Dax. I mean, I don't *dislike* you, but you know what I mean. We don't exactly get along."

"Then we won't lie," he amended. "We just hang out a couple times. We don't have to act like we're engaged or anything. Just like we're getting to know each other."

The turmoil in her stomach didn't sit well. This could get messy—what if his family found out and was hurt? But then there was that other part of her that figured it was a small thing to do to help alleviate their worrying…and they did seem concerned about Dax settling into a new town and fending for himself. They were sweet people who just wanted the best for him and he clearly worried over their distress.

This all sounded quite a bit like her own family dynamics.

"We don't have a lot of time to decide this," he added. "Since my wife passed they've just hovered over me. I needed this fresh start and now they're showing up unexpectedly and checking up on me."

He loved them, but he was frustrated. She could understand that—it was how she felt about her sisters setting her up on blind dates lately.

She knew they meant well but she needed them to back off.

"We don't know each other well," Dax continued, "but I promise, I wouldn't ask if I wasn't desperate."

That desperation came through in his tone and while she didn't know him well, she had a feeling that admission of vulnerability was difficult for him. She could also see his point of view in wanting to reassure his family this move was the right thing for him at this stage in his life. She had no idea how grief worked, but her sister had lost her own husband and had also moved in order to make a fresh start. Everyone had to work through their pain in their own way and on their own time.

Her cell chimed from the pocket of her jeans and she fished the device out and cringed when she read the text from Jenn.

A client of mine has a nephew coming in next week for a visit. He's a DOCTOR. I told her you were single and we think you two would hit it off! I know we discussed another guy earlier, but no reason you can't keep your options open!

Another blind date? Was there an end in sight?

"Everything okay?" Dax asked.

Violet glanced from her cell to him, and for

the first time in her life decided that maybe a lie wasn't always a bad thing if it was helping someone out of a tough situation.

"Another blind date?" he guessed with a lop-sided grin that sent a tingle through her belly. He leaned closer, and his masculine scent wafted over to her as he added, "That's another perk to sticking with me for two weeks."

She didn't know what she was doing, but she knew she needed a break from her family as much as he did his.

"Two weeks," she confirmed through gritted teeth. "And not a day longer."

Chapter Four

Dax had no clue why Violet changed her mind. Maybe the despair in his plea or whatever she'd seen on her phone—he wasn't sure. Regardless, a rush of relief filled him.

He'd never been one to lie and most certainly not to his family. He'd even started to correct his sister, but then his mom chimed in and then his father, and the entire situation snowballed so far out of control. And here they were.

"Thank you," he told her.

Violet held up a delicate hand in a silent gesture for him to stop.

"Is now a good time to bring up the two tickets you've given me?"

That innocent smile she offered with the sugary sweet tone had him laughing. "Are you trying to bribe an officer of the law?"

"Only if it's going to work."

Dax took his job very seriously, but he also couldn't help but admire her bold attitude and humor. He came to his feet and turned his chair to ease it under the table before focusing on Violet again. She wore no makeup and he knew she hadn't had the best of days, yet she still sat in his kitchen looking vibrant and full of life and absolutely striking. A churn of guilt stirred up his already mixed emotions.

"I'll see what I can do," he told her, trying to circle back to the situation and not this unnecessary attraction. "Now can we please just get back in there and work out details later?"

"Is this our first fight?" she asked as she stood and patted the side of his face. "We're going to need couple's counseling already."

"Very funny," he muttered, then glanced at the groceries. "Thank you for that, by the way. I didn't forget my manners—I just got caught up in my family." He crossed to the counter, putting a few items in the fridge.

"I completely understand." She sidled up to the counter and put the remaining items in the pantry. "And this fake thing is getting me out of two blind dates, so thank *you*."

He nodded. "Not a problem."

"For the record, I just brought the goods so you didn't have to get takeout or go hungry this evening or for breakfast."

"And you got a relationship in return," he replied.

"Well, it won't be for long, so I think we can do this. But in the end, we have to tell them that we realized we're better as friends."

"Absolutely." He nodded in confirmation. "I'm not looking for a relationship at all."

"At least we're on the same page. I'm not sure why our families think we need someone in our lives to complete it."

"Are you two coming back in?"

His sister's voice trailed down the hallway and Violet pursed her lips in the most adorable grin. "We're cutting some fresh bread for you all," she called back, then leaned closer to him to whisper, "Now grab a knife so I didn't just fib again."

Dax searched for a knife because he'd already forgotten which drawer he'd put his silverware in. But he stilled for a moment when he realized his hand was shaking. He'd told himself he wasn't ready for a relationship, even though his wife had been gone for three years, but perhaps this fake, temporary arrangement would be a good way to mentally ease his way into the idea.

Not that he planned on actually dating his neighbor, but if he wanted to give his parents and sister any peace of mind, Violet showing up on his doorstep seemed like the right answer at the right time. He just prayed he was doing the right thing, but since he and Violet were both on board for helping his family and not actually making this real, then he had to believe this was the logical move to make.

Violet still couldn't believe the situation she'd gotten herself into. But two weeks would fly by and then she could go back to her regular, busy life. It wasn't like she didn't have enough to do to pass the time. Thankfully Dax wasn't looking for a real relationship so they could maintain their awkward friendship—or whatever their actual status could be called. Considering they both had demanding jobs, she highly doubted they'd even see much of each other over these next fourteen days.

Vi sat in the middle of her living room floor with a variety of color-coded folders spread around her. She really hated this part of the adopt-a-thon, but the tiny details were necessary to run a smooth event. And at the end of the day, all that mattered was finding homes for lonely pets. Too many animals were dropped off unwanted or after their owners passed away. She wished she could take in each and every one, but that simply wasn't realistic.

That didn't stop her from playing Cupid with potential owners and pets. She actually loved seeing that initial connection when the right animal found the right person. It was nothing short of magical.

She glanced to her old floral sofa where her two rescues slept peacefully, snuggled against each other. As always, Stanley, her ten-year-old Saint Bernard, tucked himself in the corner and Margot, her three-year-old spaniel mix, stuck right against his plump backside. The two were like an old married couple settled in their routine and she had been wondering if she should get another. There were just so many pets she wanted and at what point did she cut herself off? Three? Five? Twelve? Self-control was difficult when it came to pets—and carbs. She loved them all.

Vi glanced back at her folders, wondering if she should address the food truck price lists or look over the pamphlets that would be passed out to each attendee with the available animals for adoption and a short bio of each. Animal bios sounded much more fun than looking at upcoming bills.

Her cell vibrated beside her and she glanced at the screen, welcoming the distraction. An unknown number popped up, but that wasn't unusual considering she got messages and calls from so many people. With a demanding job, she had to answer everything.

She shifted to a cross-legged position, swiped her finger across the screen to open the message and started reading.

I think I need a companion. Can you help me?

Vi stared at the phone, confused and a bit intrigued.

Who is this? she replied, and waited while the dots danced across the bottom of her screen.

Sorry. It's Dax. I think I need a dog. I figured you'd be the person to ask.

A chuckle escaped her and she couldn't help but shake her head in disbelief as her fingers flew over the phone.

I thought you were some obscene texter. How did you get my number? Wait. Never mind. You're the sheriff. Yeah. I can help with a dog.

Of course he had her number. She'd received two tickets since he'd gotten to town. Then again, it seemed more likely he'd asked Jack. With just a few taps, she had him added to her contacts while waiting for him to reply.

I'm not sure how this works. Haven't had a dog since I was a kid. I want something bigger. I don't care the age. My house is just too quiet.

Her heart clenched. Dax had lost his wife and Vi didn't know the circumstances or time frame.

None of that mattered. He clearly had heartache he struggled to overcome and starting over in Rosewood Valley was how he'd chosen to do that. So she would be supportive of her new… boyfriend? Gracious. This was weird and confusing. Not to mention flat-out wrong to follow through with this ruse.

But adopting out her shelter dogs came above anything right now.

I'll be at the shelter tomorrow morning if you want to stop by.

Violet already had a few dogs in mind that she thought would be a good fit for Dax. From just the little she knew of his lifestyle, he would need a well-mannered animal and likely house-or crate-trained. No matter the pet he chose, there would always be an adjustment period.

As long as nobody rear-ends me in the morning, I'll be there.

She didn't want to find him amusing. She wanted to still be annoyed, and she was for the most part, but that was a bit funny. She could have a sense of humor and find some comedic relief in the chaos of their meeting.

Vi pulled out the pamphlets for each available animal and smiled at the images and short bios.

She'd brought in a student from the local school for the photography, and she'd had her sister Erin write up a few cute sentences. This was the ultimate dating game to find the right matches.

Dutch the bulldog mix and Colt the combo of some type of wolfhound and mountain dog would be good options for Dax. Both were older and still waiting for the right person to come along. She had no doubt Dax would love one of these guys and the other would be adopted at her event. She'd followed up moments ago about the event tables and play yards and there was no doubt they would need more. She hoped their turnout was even better than last year. They'd found homes for seventeen dogs and eight cats last year, breaking their record from the year before. She was more than ready to break another record.

When her cell vibrated on the plush rug, Vi assumed she'd see Dax's name again, but her sister Rachel popped up asking if Vi could meet at the barn on Tuesday evening for a quick meeting about their next farm-to-table event.

Not long ago her family's ranch, the Four Sisters Ranch, was on the brink of foreclosure before Jenn came back into town with the brilliant idea of transforming one of their barns into an event space. Not only that, a portion of their land was sold to Jenn's now husband for him to put in his large-animal vet clinic and build a home. The ticketed farm-to-table dinners had taken off and they were busier than they ever thought possible. God had truly blessed them in so many ways. Not only had Jenn come back after being gone for years, she'd found true love once again with Luke, after the loss of her first husband. She'd also become guardian to her husband's niece, Paisley. Vi's oldest sister, Rachel, had also found love—with her childhood crush who had come to town to sell his grandfather's farm last summer but opted to stay and marry.

With all this love and happiness surrounding her, was it any wonder her family was pushing for her to join them? She and Erin weren't safe, and Vi wondered if her baby sister was also taking this heat for being single. Probably not since she was the baby of the family. Vi would find a husband one day, but she wasn't rushing anything and wanted the right man to come along so she could get to know him gradually and grow a real bond. He would have to fit into her hectic life because she would not give up her passion of saving animals and caring for the pets of Rosewood Valley.

Violet sent a quick reply to Rachel that she could be at the meeting and then she made a note on her phone so she wouldn't forget. Her schedule over the next week was about to get crazier as she was down to crunch time with her adopt-a-thon. She only had a couple short weeks to pull it together.

Vi carefully maneuvered around her folders and paperwork and came to her feet. She carefully made neat stacks and placed them on the island that separated her kitchen and living area. The movement and noise had Stanley and Margot moaning and stretching. She needed to take them out to do their business before they turned in for the night.

Stanley and Margot slid off the sofa and went straight to the back door. Their common routine made her happy. She loved her life just the way it was and couldn't imagine anything disrupting that.

Unless it was a striking yet frustrating new sheriff who needed a fake girlfriend. The situation could be seen as disruptive to some, but she wasn't going to let it cause stress or turmoil. So long as she stuck as close to the absolute truth as possible, then confessed to her family after, she would be okay. She never lied and truly didn't want to start now, but she also wanted her family to stop worrying about her— and give Dax's some peace of mind before they returned to Oregon. Her mind drifted again to the surprising man right next door. He was guarded yet vulnerable and way too handsome, and Vi wondered if their little fib would succeed in putting their families' hearts at ease— while leaving her own heart unsettled.

Chapter Five

Dax had no clue what he wanted in a dog. He hadn't owned a dog in so long, but he knew he couldn't keep coming home to a quiet house. By coming to Rosewood Valley, he'd vowed to keep putting one foot in front of the other so he could rebuild his life in whatever way God showed. He'd never relied on God more than in these last few years after June passed. He honestly didn't know how people got through difficult times without Him.

Dax pulled onto the gravel lot of the animal shelter. The old block building sat just behind Violet's animal clinic. Unlike most businesses in town, the clinic sat all on its own at the far end of the main street. The others were all attached, with bright and colorful storefronts.

The painted white building had black trim, and a black-and-white logo that read PAWS 'N' CLAWS in the front window welcomed visitors. The shelter in back looked to be an old structure, likely used for storage at one point, and Violet had transformed it for a better use. She clearly had a good heart. Not only did she care for and rescue animals, she'd also rescued him—temporarily anyway.

He still couldn't believe he'd entered into a fake relationship with a woman he barely knew. He'd told himself no relationships ever, let alone a pretend one with a virtual stranger. This might be the absolute strangest, most insane step he'd ever taken in his life. He couldn't even imagine what June was thinking as she looked down on him now. She'd likely tell him this was too drastic and just to tell the truth before he got in too deep.

Too late.

Dax rubbed the back of his neck as tension balled up like a tight fist. He'd gotten himself, and Violet, into this predicament so now he had to see it through. Two weeks would fly by and ease his parents' and sister's minds that he was going to be just fine. Worry about them also kept his mind busy and off his own heartache.

He took his radio and clipped it on his belt as he stepped from the backup patrol SUV. His was currently in the repair shop getting an estimate for the damage caused by the accident.

Gravel crunched beneath his black boots and he adjusted his Stetson to shield his eyes from the morning sun. He welcomed the warmth.

Dax had always loved summer and sunshine. He and June always vacationed somewhere tropical when they could afford a quick getaway. Now he found himself wanting a nice vacation, but going alone seemed like a waste of money and time.

The echoing of barking dogs hit him before he even opened the door. As soon as he stepped over the threshold, he spotted Violet sitting in the middle of a makeshift play area sectioned off by an octagon of what looked like baby gates. Four fluffy pups with large paws climbed over her like a human jungle gym. Dax might not know much about dogs, but he was pretty sure by the size of their paws that those dogs wouldn't stay small for long.

"Welcome to the chaos." She glanced up with a warm, inviting smile as she greeted him. "I try to work with these guys each morning. They have a ton of energy and need love."

Dax moved closer and when the pups spotted him they all swarmed toward him. Their tails wagged uncontrollably as they jumped on their back legs, eager for more attention. Their excitement was contagious and Dax found himself grinning and reaching down, trying to pet them all at once.

Violet came to her feet and swiped her hands down her blue scrubs to brush off all the dog hair. "It's going to be a gorgeous day today, so I plan on putting them out back in the fenced area to get some fresh air. I just couldn't help myself with some cuddles first."

There was no question this woman not only took her job seriously, but she found moments of joy. He rubbed between the ears of one excited dog, then another.

"How do you still have these guys?" he asked. "They seem like they'd make great pets for families."

"I agree, which is why I posted a new picture on social media this morning of all of them playing together," she stated. "They've only been here two days. They won't stay long. Everyone who comes wants puppies and the older dogs are often overlooked."

"That's a shame," he replied. "I'd think a dog that's housebroken or out of that puppy phase of chewing on everything would be more appealing."

Violet climbed over the baby gates and adjusted her high ponytail as her green gaze met his. "Everyone is different, but kids come in with the parents and instantly gravitate toward the hyper pups. Animals and people just seem to know when they've found the one."

The one. He had found the one. His person. Now she was gone. He didn't want to face that type of heartache ever again, but he also wanted someone to talk to at the end of a difficult day. A dog seemed like the best option. No back-talking, no judgment, always happy to see you. Sounded like the perfect companion for this new chapter in his life.

"So, you mentioned looking for an adult dog," she went on. "Your yard isn't fenced, so you'll need one that's disciplined as well. I already have a couple of dogs in mind, but please, if you see one that you fall in love with, that's fine. You'll know when you know."

He hoped so. He didn't care about breeds or anything like that. He cared more about giving an animal a loving home. He'd never been one to own things or associate with people for a per-fect standing or social appearances. He loved his job and his laid-back life and now he wanted to love a dog who needed a good home.

"There are a few already out back getting some playtime that you might want to check out first," Violet added.

She motioned for him to follow as she moved toward a hallway leading to the back of the building. He scanned the individual pens. Some had just one dog and a few had more. So many animals looking up at him with big eyes, silently begging for attention.

"I don't think I could do your job," he mut-tered. "I'd want to take all of them home."

She stopped and glanced over her shoulder, sending her fluffy ponytail swinging.

"Oh, it's difficult. That's why I sneak over here as much as possible from the clinic and play with them and give love. Abby, my manager for the shelter, is amazing, too. She'll bring her kids here to play and get some of the energy out of the dogs. I typically come in early and she stays late."

"Sounds like a good method." He noted a room at the end of the hall with a closed glass door. "What's in there?"

"That's the cat room," she explained. "They have a little stairway up toward the ceiling and bridge that will take them outside to a play area built above the yard so the cats get out like the dogs."

"That's pretty cool," he said, stepping closer to the door to peer inside.

"Were you also interested in a cat?" she asked. "We're overrun with them at the moment."

He turned his attention to her and shook his head. "I'm allergic, so better not."

"Oh, no." She chuckled. "I won't even open that door, then. Come on outside."

She pushed the back metal door and held it open for him. The moment they stepped out into the sunshine, several larger dogs came rushing over.

"Brace yourself," she warned with a laugh.

"They're all big babies and don't know their size."

They were instantly circled by a variety of dogs from medium to large. Some had short hair and some had thick, bushy hair. But they all had wagging tails and mouths open that made them seem as if they were smiling.

"This is going to be impossible," he stated as one massive fluffy brown canine jumped up and placed huge paws on his chest.

Dax laughed as he took a step back and held on to the paws. He didn't want to get dirt all over his uniform, but he didn't want to ignore the affection, either.

"You don't have to decide today," she informed him. "I want you and the dog to be comfortable. There's nothing worse than a dog being returned to the shelter. It confuses them and is quite traumatic."

Dax eased the dog back down to the ground and started petting a smaller copper-colored dog as he turned his head toward her.

"People return animals?" He couldn't believe such a thing happened. This wasn't a pair of shoes. This was a being with real feelings. "I just can't imagine."

Violet bent down to smooth her hand down the back of a medium-sized dog. This one appeared to be some type of beagle mix. Dax had had a beagle growing up and loved their temperament. They could be rowdy at times but often loving.

"It's maddening, quite frankly. I mean, I know not every pet works with every person, but some people return them just because they chew something or have an accident. That's part of owning a dog and there's always an adjustment period."

The passion in her tone held so much conviction. Clearly she had strong emotions about her work, which was something he could appreciate and respect.

"I assume I'll have to get some toys so I don't lose a pair of shoes," he said.

"That would be smart," she agreed as she stood back up. "Keeping things picked up and giving them appropriate things to chew on goes a long way. A new environment can make some dogs little stinkers but that's just growing pains and usually works itself out."

He nodded. "Other than work, I have nothing taking up my time so I can work with an animal."

Vi quirked a brow and crossed her arms. "You're forgetting your girlfriend."

Oh, he hadn't forgotten her. He was just trying to dodge the fact he'd placed himself smack-dab in the middle of a slight fib with a woman he barely knew.

"Yeah, well, that's short-term," he reminded her.

She smiled. "Did your parents or sister say anything after I left the other night?"

A bigger black dog with patches of white down his nose and on the tips of his ears came up to Dax with a ball in his mouth. Dax pried the wet tennis ball out and gave it a hard throw across the yard. The dog made a beeline for it.

"They really liked you." Which only caused more guilt and he wanted to come clean to them right then, but he also needed to ease their minds. "Heads up. Clara and my mother plan on asking you to lunch for a girls' day before they leave town."

Those green eyes widened for a fraction of a second, but enough for him to know that warning had stunned her.

"Don't feel obligated," he tacked on.

The dog came back with the ball and Dax gave it another toss.

"Honestly, I don't mind," she finally answered. "It will all depend on my schedule and if I can get away. But I won't avoid them. Unless this is making you uncomfortable and you need me to keep my distance."

Dax raked a hand over the back of his neck. That tension seemed to be mounting.

"I don't know what I want," he admitted. "I want them to believe I'm doing fine and I want their worry to ease. That's how I got us both into this mess."

"It's not a mess," she corrected. "You're doing me a favor as well with getting me out of blind dates with my own meddling family. Although I wouldn't have jumped right into a lie or any type of relationship, especially with you, it's not a mess and we'll be over it soon enough."

Dax stilled. "Wait. What do you mean 'especially with you'?"

Oops. Obviously she'd offended him. Well, she couldn't help her feelings. He wouldn't have been her first pick of guys to date. He wanted to adopt a dog, so he wasn't such a terrible guy, and he clearly loved his family.

But there were too many similarities between Dax and Chance that she couldn't ignore. They were both strong, determined men with a charm that pulled her in. She didn't want to be deceived ever again or be blindsided by a pretty smile and the right words.

She'd been fooled before, but her eyes were wide open now. Violet wouldn't just trust any man, no matter if he was law enforcement or not. She had to remain focused on her own life and her own happiness, at least for now until she could fully trust her judgment again.

"My family is well aware that I never want

another relationship unless I'm absolutely certain," she added. "So the fact that I'm in a relationship with a man who I thought had it in for me will give my sisters some pause."

"And why are you so against relationships?" he asked.

Violet didn't feel like getting into all of that right now. She had a patient due in about fifteen minutes and this conversation would take much longer. She didn't want to open old wounds and certainly not with Dax.

She shrugged. "Let's just say my last relationship left me evaluating a great many things, including myself."

When he started to say something else, Vi quickly changed the topic. "Anyway, as you can see there are several larger and older dogs to choose from."

Colt brought the old worn tennis ball back, always eager for a game of fetch.

"It seems as though one has taken a particular liking to you." She laughed. "This is Colt. He'd play ball all day long."

"I think he would," Dax agreed. "I'm not quite ready to make a decision, but this has given me a bit more of an understanding of what I think I'm looking for. I just need to make sure I make the right decision for not only myself, but also any dog I bring home."

Violet's heart gave a little tug. She appreciated when people took their time and made mature decisions about adopting a pet. She also knew that Dax had the purest intentions when it came to a companion. Ugh. This man did have redeeming qualities that were starting to override her irritation.

"That's fine with me," she assured him. "I have some patients coming soon but you let me know if you'd like to come back and spend more time or if you make a decision."

He gave a nod just as his radio chirped to life. She remained quiet while he listened and responded to a fender bender. Violet couldn't even suppress her smile when he focused his attention back to her.

"At least one of your patrol cars wasn't hit this time."

He propped his hands on his hips and offered a crooked grin that had her belly dancing with a bundle of nerves. She shouldn't find him so attractive and charismatic. She'd fallen for that before and all she got out of it was a shattered heart that still had some cracks. Besides, fake dating didn't require real feelings, right?

How many pep talks would she have to give herself over this man?

"Not this time," he agreed as he started back toward the door. "I'll try to distract my family from bothering you."

Violet tipped her face up to meet his gaze. "You don't have to do that. I'm busy and you're busy, so there's no need to dodge anything. If our paths cross, that's fine. I'm not afraid of family. But you should be afraid of being tackled by mine when they catch wind of this."

Dax jerked back slightly. "You think they'll find out? I haven't told anyone local."

Violet laughed. "Yeah, that's not how small towns work. You've been here long enough to know how fast the chatter spreads."

He shrugged and let out a sigh. "I hadn't thought that far."

"My family will be thrilled if they think I have a boyfriend."

Violet headed toward the door and opened it, chuckling. "Boyfriend. That's such a juvenile term for someone my age. There really should be something else."

"You think on that and let me know."

Violet laughed again and gestured him inside. The chaos in the shelter matched that outside and she hated leaving all the pups, but she had to be at her clinic for the next several hours. This was her long workday, coming in at well over eight hours. Good thing she loved her job.

"I'll text you about the dog," he told her as he reached the front door. "I'll stop on my way home and get some necessary things like a leash, collar, chew toys."

"Always good to have that in place," she agreed. "And depending on the dog, I can give you food recommendations. A couple of our resident canines have a food allergy."

"Good to know. Thanks for meeting me."

The way his bold blue eyes held hers had her stomach forming knots once again. She needed the next two weeks to fly by so she could distance herself. She'd only been around the man for a couple of days and already her emotions were all over the place. Her heart couldn't take another attachment and she wasn't looking for anything anyway. Neither was Dax. He'd made that clear and she couldn't blame him. The loss of the love of your life had to be a traumatic experience, and from what he'd told her, he was here for a fresh start. Nothing more.

She imagined once they were done with this ruse they wouldn't see much of each other. Even though they were neighbors, they did have a good-sized field between their houses and no reason to speak to each other. She didn't figure they had much in common, aside from the meddling families they were hoping to put at ease, so there wouldn't be a reason to see him, right?

The front door opened and both Dax and Violet jerked back as if they'd been caught doing something. Which was ridiculous. Her guilt was already making her edgy and they'd barely begun this charade.

Violet glanced beyond Dax to the familiar boy with brown hair and dark eyes in the doorway. "Hey, Oliver. I wasn't expecting you today."

The twelve-year-old who lived just a half mile away would often walk over and help wherever she needed. She knew Oliver had faced his share of struggles as a foster child, and she hoped by giving him this outlet she could give him a little bit of hope and light for his future and show him that people did actually care. She noted the camera bag on his shoulder, but he didn't come in any farther. In fact, his eyes traveled between her and Dax.

"I can come back tomorrow if that's better," Oliver stated, his eyes locking back on Dax.

"I was just leaving," Dax informed him, then extended his hand. "I'm Dax Adams."

Oliver was hesitant, but ultimately reached out and shook the sheriff's hand. "Oliver Edwards."

"He volunteers several hours a week here," Violet said. "He actually took all of the pictures for the pamphlets we'll be passing out at Pets in the Park. Oliver has a great eye for detail."

The boy dropped his head, clearly embarrassed by the compliment. That was another thing. She was trying to get him to communicate better and be proud of all the positives he had in his life.

Violet knew his foster parents and he was in such good hands; she only hoped he continued on that path, and she would do everything she could to help guide him during their time together.

"I asked him to come by sometime to take pictures of the animals playing together so I can use them for social media," she told Dax.

"If you're too busy now—" Oliver began.

"Now is fine," she insisted. "Abby will be here shortly and I'll be over at the clinic. I know nothing about photography so you won't need me here anyway. You've been here enough to know to keep the kennels closed and locked."

Oliver nodded.

"I need to go, too." Dax started toward the door and eased by Oliver. "It was nice meeting you."

Oliver nodded. "You, too."

"I'll walk him out and be right back in," she told Oliver as she followed Dax.

As the shelter door swung closed, she fell into step with Dax.

"Oliver is one of the foster kids I have come in for a few hours a week," she told him. "There are some who have a tendency to get into trouble at school so I was hoping that by giving them a positive outlet and some responsibility, they would make a turn."

Dax stopped at the patrol car he had to use temporarily.

"That's remarkable," he told her as he slid his hat off. He opened the car door and tossed the Stetson onto the passenger seat. "You really do try to save everyone around you, don't you?"

Violet shrugged. "I don't know about that, but I think everyone deserves a good life."

His radio came to life again and Dax listened as he eased behind the wheel.

"Let me know if you need help choosing anything for your new pet," she told him once the radio chatter stopped. She took a step back so he could close the door. "See you at the council fundraiser."

"See you there."

The black-and-white patrol car pulled away and Violet let out a sigh, wondering why she watched until the vehicle was out of sight and the dust had settled back down onto the gravel. She shouldn't take any other interest in him. As of just a few days ago he irked her, then suddenly they needed each other's help and she found him moderately intriguing.

She didn't like these unexpected emotions and she certainly didn't have time for them. If she just remained focused on her work, her family and her adopt-a-thon, she wouldn't have to worry about unnecessary thoughts. She'd be too preoccupied with what mattered and all of her long-term relationships—not this short-term situation.

Chapter Six

"I understand, Mrs. Downing, but we're a small department and we can't just have a deputy sitting on your street to see who is stealing your newspaper."

The conversations Dax overheard from the dispatcher typically amused him. Of course there were serious issues the department had to address, but as a small town they didn't have too many traumatic problems. Minor inconveniences, like missing newspapers—or getting rear-ended by a beautiful vet.

When he'd stopped by her shelter this morning, he hadn't anticipated finding so many precious dogs who needed homes. And he certainly hadn't anticipated seeing just how amazing Violet was in her element. There wasn't a doubt in his mind she devoted every bit of her energy into loving those animals in need. She'd created quite a sanctuary for them, but part of him wondered who made a sanctuary for her?

She'd indicated she'd been left before, and he hadn't missed the pain in her voice, but she hadn't wanted to talk about it. Honestly, he didn't want to talk about his pain, either. He couldn't imagine opening up to anyone like he had with June.

His cell vibrated in his pocket just as he reached his office door. He pulled the device out and stared at the message on the screen.

This is so ironic. Someone just popped in and asked about Colt. There's no pressure for you to take him but I thought you should know since you were just here.

What were the odds? He did really like Colt, but was that the dog for him? Dax wasn't sure. He wanted to see the dog one more time but didn't know when their schedules would align again.

His thumbs moved over the screen as he sent back a quick reply.

Is there any chance I can come see him later today? If you can't hold him, I understand. Do what is best for the dog.

She immediately started typing back so he waited. Staring at his screen like some six-teen-year-old was new to him when it came to a woman. He hadn't done this since June, but he blamed his anxious state on the dog and not the woman.

I'd much rather Colt go to you if you'd like. I think you two are a good fit and it would be a legit relationship…not like ours.

Dax chuckled as he pushed open the door to his office. He stepped in and stopped short when Clara smiled from behind his desk. With her booted feet propped on the edge, she laced her fingers over her abdomen.

"Smiling at your phone like someone in love. You must be texting Violet."

Dax gripped his cell in one hand and entered the room. He certainly wasn't in love, and just because he was smiling didn't mean anything. He smiled at friends all the time. Violet had made a joke, that was all. And Clara was seeing exactly what he'd wanted her to—that he was happy and at peace with his new life.

"What are you doing here?" he asked.

"Thought I'd surprise you."

Dax laughed as he shut the door behind him. "Oh, I'm surprised, but did you need me?"

"Just wanted to see your space and check on you," she explained, making no effort to move.

"Hope you don't mind I took your seat. It's a tiny office."

"Tiny town," he replied, resting a hip on the edge of his desk. "Did you really just stop to see me or were you trying to get a breather from our parents?"

The smirk on his sister's face gave him the answer he needed.

"I hope you at least have your own room at the B and B," he added.

"Oh, that was a must for this trip," she confirmed. "I love them, you know that. They're just a bit pushy at times. They're loving this town, by the way, and we've only been here two days."

"They moving here?" he joked.

Clara dropped her feet to the floor and leaned forward as she held his gaze. "No, but they've hinted I'd find a nice man here and already asked where the closest hospital was for me to look into transferring."

Dax's gut tightened. Had his parents already moved on from worrying about him so that they were focusing on Clara? That meant his plan was working.

"Are you looking for a move or a man?" he asked casually.

She rolled her eyes and let out the most unladylike snort. "Not hardly. I like my life in Oregon and my job. I'm actually up for a promotion in about six months so I don't want to miss that chance. And as far as a man goes, if God wants me to be married, He'll send someone my way. And by that I mean I need a clear sign because sometimes I'm oblivious."

The tap on his door had Dax turning his attention from his twin to see who the visitor was.

"Come in," he called.

The door opened with a slow creak and one of his deputies, Ben, stepped in. The tall, young deputy with cropped dark hair offered an apologetic smile.

"Sorry to interrupt," he stated, then his eyes darted around the small room and landed on Clara.

Dax glanced over his shoulder to see Clara staring right back and Dax had to suppress his grin. Was this God plopping someone right in front of her? The timing couldn't be more ironic and Ben was a single man. But no way was Dax going to start playing matchmaker. He had enough relationship, temporary as it may be, going on to worry about the personal lives of an employee and his sister.

"No interruption," Dax stated as he came to his feet. "This is my twin sister, Clara. She and my parents came to town for a visit."

Clara was up and around the desk in record

time as she extended her hand. "Nice to meet you."

"Likewise. I'm Ben," he said, taking her hand.

The eye contact those two shared had Dax wondering if he was an instant third wheel. Instead of wallowing in this uncomfortable tension in the closet-sized space, Dax cleared his throat.

"What's up?" Dax asked.

Ben dropped his hand and glanced at Dax. "Oh, I just needed to discuss taking a few days off next week. My dad is having surgery and my mother can't drive so I just wanted to see if I can be available for them or if I need to find someone else to take him."

Dax knew enough about Ben's mother to know she was legally blind and her husband took her everywhere. The couple was always seen around town at the grocery or the bank. They were quite adorable.

"That won't be a problem," Dax said. "Family first. We'll be fine here."

Ben nodded. "I appreciate that. I'll let you two get back to your visit." He tipped his hat toward Clara. "Nice to meet you, ma'am."

The deputy stepped back out the door and shut it with a soft click.

When Dax shifted and looked at his sister, she remained staring at the closed door.

"Do I need to give you his number?"

Clara blinked and jerked like she'd just woken from some daydream. "What? No. Of course not. I'm not staying in town, remember? My promotion?"

"Oh, I remember, but you also said God had to put someone in your path and a second later Ben knocked on the door and now you have the same look you had in high school when Dylan Parker asked you to prom."

Clara swatted his arm. "I most certainly do not. I'm a grown woman, not a teen with a crush. And Dylan turned out to be a nightmare date when he tripped going into the restaurant and grabbed my dress and tore the sleeve off."

Dax couldn't prevent the laughter that bubbled up and out. "I forgot about that. Your pictures from that night were hilarious."

Clara's eyes narrowed as she glared at him. "You would think that was funny. Mom and I shopped forever trying to find the perfect dress and that klutz ruined it."

"Well, if it helps, he's married with kids now and off the market, so you have nothing to worry about."

"Yeah, I know." Clara sighed and tucked her long blond hair behind her ears. "Anyway, I didn't come here to find a man. I came to see if you needed help with your house tonight. I was waiting on you to text us and let us know how we could help, but you haven't asked in the two days we've been here. Maybe you've been busy with Violet?"

Not really. And the ball of guilt in his gut tightened. He planned on sticking to the truth as much as possible—that he and Violet were busy and couldn't spend too much time together with their demanding careers. That certainly wasn't a lie.

"She's pretty swamped with her clinic and no-kill animal shelter," he replied. "I saw her this morning when I went to look for a dog, but other than that I haven't seen her since the other night when you met."

There. One hundred percent the truth.

"A dog?" Clara repeated with a soft tone. "Oh, that would be so perfect for you and that nice big yard you have. Did you get one?"

"Not yet." Dax eased by his sister and opted to take a seat at his own desk since she'd vacated the old leather chair. "There was one that kept playing ball with me and I liked him, but I need to think and pray on this because I want it to be a good fit for not only me but the dog also."

"That dog will be grateful to have you. Are you sure you can juggle your new career and a pet?"

Dax nodded. "That's what Violet was helping me with this morning. The dog's housebroken and I can fence in part of the yard and leave him out for a bit if I need."

Clara smiled. "Sounds like Violet is going to be beneficial to you in more than one area."

If Clara only knew just how beneficial Violet had already been.

"I actually need to get to some reports," he told his sister, before she could dive any deeper. "Did you need anything else?"

Clara glanced around the office and stopped short at the black-and-white photo hanging near the one and only window. She crossed the small space and stood staring.

"You look like him," she mused.

Dax had been told that more than once. His great-great-grandfather had been the first sheriff of Rosewood Valley and until Dax came to town, no one else in the family had taken this position. Dax was proud of his heritage and pleased when the photo was already on display when he arrived. He could admit he saw some resemblance—and it was pretty neat to have this heritage.

"He'd be proud of you, knowing one of his descendants has taken over." Clara spun back around to face him. "I'm really glad you made this move. I think it will be good for you in so many ways."

Yeah. He really did, too… Now he just needed his family to trust in that.

"I'll let you get back to work." Clara pulled her key from her pocket and moved toward the door. "I think I'll stop by that cute little coffee shop and maybe find a thrift store to get you a housewarming gift."

"Is this going to be like that tacky wedding gift you got for me and June?" He laughed.

Clara crossed her arms. "For your information, that owl lamp was a beautiful statement piece."

"Shame it broke on my move here."

Her gaze narrowed once again. "Oh, I'll find something equally as beautiful. See you, baby brother."

Dax blew out a breath as he leaned forward in his seat. The creaking echo of the old leather chair filled the small space and he wiggled his mouse to wake his computer. The last thing he wanted to do was work on reports. He wanted to go shopping for canine toys and bedding, and then head back to the shelter to visit the dogs once again.

And maybe he wanted to see Violet. He shouldn't let that unwanted pull drag him back, but something about her intrigued him. She was refreshing and bold. He hadn't been interested in a woman in a long time and he wasn't interested in her romantically so much as curious to get to know her. Strictly on a friendship level, though. Nothing more. Just someone to talk to, maybe share some jokes with or a meal every now and then. There wasn't anything wrong with that—right?

Violet pulled up to the barn that had been transformed from livestock housing into event space a year ago. When Jenn had come back home after years away and suggested they have farm-to-table dinners for special occasions and charge per person as a way to help save the farm, her family jumped into action. Not only did that act save the farm, but the family once again became unified. Now they worked together with each event and this particular event they were doing next just so happened to be put on by none other than Dax, as a fundraiser for the town council.

She got out of her car and quickened her step as a drizzle of rain started falling. The gray skies didn't look too promising, but at least the event wasn't until Saturday afternoon and hopefully they could keep the barn doors open and have a lovely flow of entertaining indoors and out.

The moment she stepped through the side door and shook the moisture from her hair and face she looked up—and noticed all eyes were on her.

Jenn, Rachel and Erin all stood near the closest round dinner table as if they'd been waiting on her arrival.

"What?" Violet asked. "Am I late?"

"You're late in telling us you're dating the sheriff," Jenn stated.

Vi's stomach knotted as a lump formed in her throat. She had planned on discussing this whole situation with them in person, but she hadn't expected them to know already. Of course, she should have been prepared for just that, though. Rosewood Valley wasn't known for keeping secrets and any type of exciting news, especially about the town's most eligible bachelor, would spread rapidly.

Goodness.

"I was going to tell you," she began, stepping farther into the space. "I just wanted to do it in person. I figured if I messaged on the family text that you all would show up on my doorstep."

And they would.

Sticking as close to the truth as possible was the only way she'd get through this farce. She didn't want to feel guilty for helping out a... friend? Was Dax a friend? No, they weren't anywhere close to that status. They were neighbors, helping each other out by doing neighborly things. Which in this case included helping him find a dog—and pretending to date him for the benefit of his family.

They clearly cared for him and he wanted to start a new life where he could move beyond his pain. She couldn't fault him, and he'd asked for her help. He was helping her, too—when her family saw her show up to Dax's event on his arm, maybe they'd get the message that she wasn't on the market for more blind dates.

"Is that right?" Rachel asked.

Violet set her keys and phone on one of the undecorated tables by the door and adjusted her ponytail. "Promise," she assured them. "I didn't feel this was for a text and I've been busy finalizing things for Pets in the Park and then I met with Dax's family—"

"Wait." Erin held up her hand. "You met his family? Isn't that moving really fast? Don't they live out of town?"

"Did they come in just to meet you?" Rachel asked.

Violet shook her head. "No, no. Nothing like that. They were already in town to visit Dax and see his new house. They hadn't visited since his move. I just happened to drop by and they were there so I met them."

"You baked for him?" Erin asked, her brows raised so high her forehead had rows of wrinkles.

Violet had a sinking feeling this wouldn't be

nearly as easy as she'd thought. She was starting to dig herself a deeper hole. The way the words just came tumbling out of her mouth made this entire situation seem much more serious than the reality.

"I was baking bread for my new neighbor," she explained. "I had no idea it was Dax."

"You're dating and you didn't know he was the one moving in next to you?" Jenn chimed in.

Violet crossed her arms and sighed. "Listen, I said everything was new. We've literally only been talking a few days."

There. That was one hundred percent the truth. She hadn't even met Dax before she'd rear-ended him even though he'd been in town for a couple months.

"We need all the details." Rachel picked up a stack of sage-green napkins. "But we have to work while we talk. These tables won't decorate themselves."

Violet hoped she could shift the topic to something, *anything*, else. She doubted it, but that didn't mean she couldn't be hopeful. She went to the closet at the back of the barn where they kept the clean tablecloths draped and ready to go. Maybe if she took her time and pulled them out one by one, they'd forget this chatter about Dax.

"Are you stalling over there?" Jenn's question echoed through the spacious two-story space.

Violet slid a cloth off a hanger and draped it over her arm before turning and heading back to her sisters. "Why would I be stalling?" she asked with a smile. "If anyone else wants to grab more tablecloths, we could get this done a bit faster."

"I'm more interested in getting the how-you-met-Dax story done faster," Erin muttered.

Rachel snickered, and Violet shot her sister a look, but Rachel merely shrugged as if she wasn't sorry one bit.

"I promised Paisley I'd help her with a school project so I can't stay more than an hour to help decorate," Jenn told them. "Sorry. But I can come back in the morning before I open the shop and do any touching up that needs doing."

Jenn wasn't just a salon owner and newly-wed—she'd also taken on the role of mother to her husband's niece, whom Luke had been given guardianship of when Paisley's parents had been tragically killed in an auto accident. Jenn, Luke and Paisley had all found each other and they were growing beautifully together as a family. Not to mention the stray dog, Cookie, that had wandered into their lives. They all blended perfectly and Violet couldn't imagine a better fit.

"What kind of project?" Violet asked, shifting a few of the chairs to make room for more. They'd hoped the entire town would turn out for their biggest event at the farm to date. The

RSVP list was quite large so she had to believe this would be a huge success.

"No." Erin took the tablecloth and gave it a soft flick to send it flaring over one of the tables. "You're not moving this conversation to another topic."

Of course she wouldn't get off that easy. Violet decided to just give them some information and then move on. That was all she could do.

"We met for the first time when I smashed into the back of his patrol car," she admitted honestly.

Silence filled the area and she met the stunned stare of each of her sisters. Violet waited, but nobody said a word.

"You're making that up," Rachel finally stated.

"Afraid not." Violet smoothed her hands over the freshly placed tablecloth. "Maybe smashed is too harsh of a term, but I hit him and now we both have our cars in the body shop. In my defense, I was belting out my favorite song that we sing at church and next thing I know I'm jerking to a stop. Metal crunched against metal and I met the new sheriff in the worst possible way."

Violet cringed as the day replayed in her mind. "Needless to say it was an awkward encounter and I got yet another ticket. Once I got home, I saw a moving truck next door and I whipped up some banana bread and took it over. We got to

talking and agreed to keep seeing each other...
And that brings you all up to date."

And dodged the rest of the little fib she wanted
to skirt around.

"There has to be more." Jenn came back
with more cloths for the bare tables and Rachel
grabbed one of the drapes off the top. "You've
been against dating anyone since you-know-who
and now suddenly you're dating the most high-
profile eligible bachelor in town."

Violet chewed the inside of her cheek. Her
sisters were her very best friends and she never
wanted to deceive them. She never *had* deceived
them. She'd also promised Dax this favor while
his parents and sister were in town.

"For now, we're just keeping things between
us and figuring everything out since it's all so
new," Violet admitted.

Three sets of eyes stared back at her and she
knew without a doubt each sister had a whole
host of questions, but thankfully none of them
said a word. Violet let out a sigh of relief. They'd
be able to see right through her if she didn't
sound and act convincing. Nobody knew her
better except her parents, so they'd be the next
hurdle to jump. The thought of keeping up this
ruse with her parents made her second-guess her
decision. Would they be hurt if they found out

the truth? And yet she wanted to help Dax—not to mention herself.

She took a deep breath. "Please, don't bombard him with questions when he's here for the event," she begged. "He's the sheriff, first and foremost. The night is to raise money for the town and it's Dax's first event in this role. Not to mention his family is in town."

"We would never corner someone like that," Erin stated, then thumbed to her right. "Well, Rachel might."

"Hey," Rachel scoffed. "I take offense to that. I will be on my best behavior."

Violet sincerely hoped so. She knew her family's business meant everything to them, but she also knew how nosy they were, especially when it came to relationships.

A familiar chime from her purse cut through their working atmosphere and Violet dropped her tablecloth to get to her phone. She never knew when an animal was in a state of emergency and never wanted to leave a client hanging.

The instant she pulled out her cell, she realized it was a message from Dax. She swiped her fingertip across the screen and the moment his text opened, an image appeared. Violet gasped, her hand coming up to her mouth as she took in the sight.

"What is it?" Rachel asked. "Is everything okay?"

Her sister started making her way over, followed by Erin and Jenn. Violet glanced up to worried stares from all three siblings. She let out a laugh and turned her phone around for them to see. It was a photo of Dax grinning next to Colt. The dog was also looking at the camera, nestled right up against Dax.

"Dax just sent this to me," she told them. "Isn't it the cutest?"

Her sisters moved in closer to get a better look.

"He came by the shelter earlier this morning and was thinking about adopting a dog," Violet explained. "He played with Colt, this guy here in the picture, and then I told him this afternoon that someone else was interested in the dog and Dax was going to try to go back sometime to visit him."

She turned the cell back so she could look at the image once again. Another message popped up.

Abby was here and let me visit Colt. Thought you'd want to see that we still get along.

"Look at that smile on her face," Jenn muttered. "I've never seen her smile like that to anyone."

Violet couldn't help herself. She wasn't going

to pretend this picture didn't bring her pure joy. The happiness on both Dax's and Colt's faces was great. She didn't know how he'd done it, but this selfie was one of the most precious things she'd ever seen.

"I'm just so happy that they found each other," Violet explained as she started to type a response.

I love this! Did you take him home?

"Do you always get this excited about adoptions?" Erin asked.

Violet shrugged. "Usually. Knowing my animals are going to a good home is the best feeling. And Dax needs a companion. I think this will be one of my favorite pairings."

"More than you and him?" Rachel questioned. "Because you seem pretty happy right now."

Yeah. She was. This one silly little picture brightened her day and gave her a sense of warmth that she hadn't expected from Dax. All she could attribute this to was that he'd made a decision and there would be one less animal sleeping in a kennel.

"I am happy," Violet replied.

Minus the tiny lie she and Dax carried around with them.

Another message popped up and she glanced back down.

Not today. I want him but I'd have to get everything ready. Maybe a couple of days.

A couple of days was fine. Violet would help him with whatever he needed, and she would gladly help with that transition. Anything to aid in the union of two lonely souls healing each other.

"Be honest."

Violet dropped her phone on the table and focused on Rachel. Did she already know the truth?

"About what?" Violet asked.

"Does Dax make you smile and love life?" Rachel leaned her hip on the back of a chair. "Because I was starting to worry about you. Jenn and I were racking our brains trying to think of dates—"

Violet sighed. "Yes, I'm aware."

Jenn winced. "Sorry. It's just that we love you and want you happy. You and Erin."

"Oh, no." Erin waved her hands. "Leave me out of this. Don't start finding dates for me."

Violet felt bad for her sister, but hey, if Rachel and Jenn weren't bugging Vi, then…

She only hoped when she told them the truth that they'd let the subject drop and believe she was happy on her own with her life just the way it was. Violet wasn't so sure that would actually happen, but she had some time to prepare a convincing speech. What mattered in the end was that Dax's family had peace knowing he had found comfort in his life here. Everything would be just fine—so long as she didn't get her emotions tangled up in this situation.

Chapter Seven

❧

"Are you still able to order more ferns?"

Violet leaned on the checkout counter that stretched across the front of All Good Things as Rachel eased up onto the stool. Erin had stopped by a while ago, but the place had been packed. A very good problem to have, considering the local feedstore had been in some financial trouble not long ago.

"Sure," Rachel replied. "How many more do you need? Are these for your house?"

"No, they're for Pets in the Park," Violet informed her. "I'd like to have them placed on each side of the steps leading to the stage in the gazebo where the podium will be set up. Or do you think that's too much?"

"I think that would look nice," Rachel replied.

The chime on the entrance pulled Violet's attention to the wide open barn doors. She straightened and smiled as Dax's father stepped in.

"Good evening," Violet greeted as she took a

step toward him. "What are you doing out and about?"

Mike Adams turned toward her and the genuine smile that spread across his face warmed her heart. An instant image of what Dax would look like in thirty years stood before her.

Violet pulled in a deep breath and pushed aside thoughts of future Dax. There was no need to wonder about that because she had no intention of moving beyond this little arrangement they currently had.

"I had to run to the store for Kay and on my way I saw the potted flowers out front, so I just thought I'd swing in on my way back through."

"You certainly came to the right place for beautiful flowers," Violet assured him.

She turned and pointed toward her sister, who was moving around the checkout counter and coming toward them.

"This is one of my sisters, Rachel," Violet introduced. "She and her husband own this store and she does all the ordering."

Mike glanced over Violet's shoulder and gave a nod in greeting. "It's nice to meet you," he said extending his hand.

Violet took a step back so the two could shake hands. "Rachel, this is Dax's father, Mike."

"Oh, really." Rachel's arched brows shot up. "Well, it's lovely to meet you."

The turmoil swirling in Violet's belly intensified as her sister seemed all too eager to meet Mike. Violet didn't want the families to intermingle any more than necessary. The sooner she and Dax could go back to their single lives, the better for both of them.

"Can I get a couple of those pots?" he asked. "I think they'd look nice on Dax's new front porch."

"That sounds like a lovely housewarming present," Rachel agreed. "I'll get you rung up right over here and then help you load your car."

"I'll actually put them in mine," Violet found herself chiming in before she could think. "I'm heading that way anyway and you said you just got groceries, right? No need to crush anything."

She needed to head home anyway, and she also wondered if Dax needed help warding off questions and his family, who he felt could be smothering at times.

"That would be wonderful." He reached for his back pocket and pulled out his wallet. "Kay and Clara will be so happy to see you."

He handed his credit card to Rachel just as another customer walked in. Rachel gave them a quick greeting and then focused back on Mike.

"Just getting two?" she asked.

"That will work. Violet, go ahead and choose whichever you think my son would like."

Uh…how would she know what he liked? She just met her new "boyfriend" only a few days ago.

"Sure thing," she confirmed. "I'll go do that right now."

She turned to her sister before she headed out the door. "Let me know when those ferns come in and I'll swing by."

Rachel waved a hand. "No. You have enough you're dealing with. I'll bring them for Pets in the Park."

Violet sighed. "Thank you. I'll let you get back to work and I'll go grab those flowers."

"See you at the house," Mike called after her.

As Violet stepped from the store, she thought for sure she heard Mike comment on what a cute couple she and Dax were.

With a guilty conscience, Violet chose bright yellow flowers, hoping Dax would approve. In offering to bring them, she'd just wanted to continue to support him and take some pressure off him from his family. But maybe she was just getting everyone in deeper than necessary.

"I don't know what to wear to the town fundraiser."

"I guess I could wear that nice blouse with my jeans and boots."

"The one with the polka dots? That would be pretty, but I'm afraid this event is fancier than jeans. Sounds like a good reason to go shopping."

"We never *need* a reason to go shopping."

The chatter between his mother and his sister hit him the moment he opened the back door. Dax barely resisted the urge to turn and walk back out. Shopping certainly wasn't a topic he loved diving into, especially after a long day. He'd just gotten off work and hadn't expected his family to be at his house, but he wasn't surprised and he certainly wouldn't turn down a home-cooked meal. He was terrible in the kitchen, not to mention cooking for one seemed like too much work, especially after putting in a ten-hour shift.

"Ladies, you can wear anything you want to the event," he interjected as he closed the door behind him and moved into the kitchen. "Many women will be dressed up, but nothing too fancy about Rosewood Valley. Jeans will be perfectly fine."

His mother turned from peeling an apple and smiled. "Dax, I didn't even hear you come in."

"Because you two are worried about your wardrobe," he muttered as he crossed the room to kiss his mother and sister on the cheek. He hadn't forgotten his manners.

"We just don't want to embarrass the new sheriff," Clara told him as she covered another pork chop in a heavy coating of flour. "We're a representation of you and our family history is deep in this town. Besides, a fundraiser for the town council sounds dressy."

Dax laughed. "You guys won't embarrass me. But if you really want to dress up, there are a couple of ladies' shops in town you might like."

"Why don't you go change." His mom's attention turned back to her peeling. "We're having fried pork chops, scalloped potatoes, cooked apples and coleslaw. Your father just ran to the store because I didn't get all I needed earlier. I always tell myself I'll remember and it never happens."

Dax nodded and headed from the kitchen toward the staircase. As he reached the first step, his cell vibrated in his pocket. He pulled out the phone and a message from Rachel Spencer Hart popped on the screen.

Does everything look okay to you? Whatever you don't like can be changed!

The next message was a video of the venue and the open barn area with multiple round tables decorated in white and green from the chair coverings to the tablecloths and the floral arrangements. Everything looked classy yet casual at the same time. The space was quite a transformation from the empty barn he'd toured with Rachel when booking the date and getting ideas for food and setup.

Everything Rachel and her sisters had done was perfect for the event he wanted to host as the new sheriff. Not only was this a big fund-raiser for the town council, but it was also the perfect opportunity for him to say thank-you to the town for the huge welcome they'd given him.

Dax watched the video through once more. He knew nothing about decorating, but he knew Four Sisters was the only place to hold such an important occasion and there hadn't been any doubt they would pull off something magnificent. He'd trusted they knew what they were doing and this was all perfect.

He'd dealt with Rachel through this entire ordeal and she'd been amazing. Not to mention her husband, Jack Hart, who had been the one to find Dax this house. He really did feel so at home here in Rosewood Valley and couldn't wait for the opportunity to show his gratitude.

He just hoped things didn't get weird with Violet and his family together. They could pull this off. They didn't have to be affectionate or put on any type of fake showing. That wasn't what this event was about. There would be enough people there to keep him distracted enough that he wouldn't have to be with Violet. She was much too distracting as it was, with her attractive girl-next-door looks and her mesmerizing swinging ponytails.

Dax pushed thoughts of Violet aside and focused on the message from her sister. He shot off a quick, thankful reply.

Everything looks great. I had no doubt. Thank you.

He headed on up to the main suite of his new home. Boxes still lined some of the hallway and the rooms. His cell vibrated again before he reached the top.

And congrats on dating my sister and taking her off the market. You got a good one.

He stared at the message, having no clue how to respond. "Thank you" seemed odd and he didn't know what conversation Violet had had with her sisters. Instead, he slid the cell back into his pocket. He'd have to talk to Violet privately and find out what she'd said so he didn't say the wrong things.

Dax took another step, but just as he hit the top of the landing, he stilled. The paint fumes hit him first. He certainly hadn't painted, which could only mean one thing. He glanced into the spare bedroom and noted the once gray walls were now a pale blue.

No doubt Clara had done that while he'd been

gone because that room was most definitely gray when he'd left at five thirty this morning.

Dax remained in the doorway and stared as if he could somehow flip the shade back to what it was simply by remaining in place. But no. The color was blue, similar to the bathroom June had done before she'd passed.

He would talk to Clara. There would have to be some boundaries. He couldn't have his new house completely reminding him of all he'd lost. Remembering was one thing, but wallowing in the past was another.

As much as this interference irritated him, he couldn't be too angry. If his family wanted to help him settle in, so be it. He knew this came from a place of love. He just wanted them to stay out of his love life—or lack thereof. He wasn't looking, nor did he feel the need to force something into a space that simply wouldn't fit.

Dax headed on into his room, thankful it was still a nice shade of off-white. He quickly changed his clothes and gathered up his dirty uniform to put in the wash.

Once he had that all set, he moved back through his sparsely furnished room and paused. He had a feeling he should tell Clara this one was off-limits. He liked the simplicity of the white walls, the dark wood floors and having no curtains so he could see out back into his own private yard. He didn't need any frills or fancy artwork or mounds of throw pillows. He'd even gotten a new bed for the move. He'd needed to start completely fresh. But as he turned toward the doorway, his gaze landed on the single photo on the chest of drawers. The one photo he'd kept in his room in the old house and now in this one.

The wedding picture of him and Junie taken just outside the church beneath the old oak tree. She had her head back, laughing, and he honestly couldn't recall what he'd said to bring that wide smile to her face, but he could still hear that sweet laughter. And even though he was moving on and starting fresh, he never wanted to forget. He kept telling himself she would be proud of him for this transition, so he kept her beautiful, smiling face right here so he'd see the reminder each and every morning.

Dax made his way back to the steps and voices filtered up from the first floor. His father had clearly returned from his errand. Dax hadn't made any of his own memories yet in this house, so he was glad the first ones were with his parents and sister. Maybe God knew what He was doing when He sent them on that exact day.

Actually, there was no maybe about it. God always knew what Dax needed before Dax ever knew.

The moment he moved through the doorway

from the hallway into the kitchen, all eyes turned to him and conversation ceased. The silence settled into the room like an unwelcome fifth member to their party.

"What is it?" he asked. He could tell nothing was actually wrong, not with their goofy grins. But he didn't like the way all eyes were on him and his gut tightened.

"Just a little present for you on the front porch," his father stated with that silly grin like he was hiding a secret.

"You're being weird," Dax stated. "All of you. What's on my porch?"

"Go take a look," his mom stated as she went back to working on dinner.

Dax had no clue what to expect, but he made his way toward the foyer. The moment he swung open the door, Violet jumped back with a hand to her chest as her eyes met his.

"Oh, Dax. You startled me."

He paused, taking in the sight of Violet in her gray scrub pants and simple T-shirt with her clinic logo on the front and her hair in a high ponytail. But it was the potted flowers that caught his attention.

"You randomly dropped by to put flowers on my porch?" he joked as he stepped toward her. The door shut behind him, hopefully blocking out anyone who might want to eavesdrop.

"Actually this was your dad's idea," she countered as she glanced down to the bright yellow buds. "I was at the feedstore talking to Rachel when he stopped by. He thought your porch needed a bit more."

Dax snorted. "More likely my mother told him my porch was boring and to find something colorful. So how did you get roped into making the delivery?"

"Actually I volunteered." She shifted her attention back to him and shrugged. "I wondered how you were doing. And if we should keep appearances."

Something stirred within Dax—something he couldn't quite put his finger on. But the fact she'd thought of him really warmed his heart. She'd likely worked all day and still helped his father at the feedstore and then was selfless enough to put him and his family ahead of heading on home.

He shouldn't allow the sweet gesture to sway him toward anything other than being thankful. He hadn't asked her to pretend with him so he could use that as a stepping stone to anything more.

"Thank you," he told her, trying to keep everything still on that friend level…or perhaps this was more like a business transaction. Regardless, he owed her a thank-you every chance he got.

"No problem at all." She tipped her head,

sending her ponytail shifting over one slender shoulder, then offered a smile. "Everything going good?"

"So far. My mom and sister are making dinner. I'm sure they'll have my whole house decorated before they leave town," he joked.

Violet winced. "Is that something you want?" When he didn't respond, she added, "Should you tell them that's something we're doing together or is that taking this too far?"

Considering his family hadn't crossed the line yet and tried to overtake everything, he'd stay quiet. Yet again, Violet was putting herself out there for him, and he liked the feeling. He wasn't naive. Dax was well aware she was in this to help keep her own family from breathing down her neck with dates and asking when she'd settle down.

Violet didn't have to do anything extra, yet here she was doing just that.

"I don't think you need to do any damage control," he said, "but thanks for the offer." He gestured toward the flowers. "And thanks for those."

"It was your dad," she repeated.

"I'm sure you picked them out. I wouldn't have thought about putting anything out here. June always did things like that."

And she would definitely approve of yellow… and quite possibly Violet.

The instant that thought popped into his mind, he had to push it aside. Nothing more was coming from this arrangement and in no time at all, they'd be back to their regularly scheduled lives.

"Well, I'm going to head home unless there's anything more you'd like me to do," she offered.

"You're good, but you might want to head out before my family comes out and ushers you in for dinner." He laughed, surprised they hadn't done that yet.

Violet's wide eyes were the only indication she wasn't too keen on a family dinner, and he didn't blame her. That was something neither of them were prepared for.

"I'll tell them you had to get home to feed your dogs or work on the adopt-a-thon," he told her, giving her an easy out.

She nodded and started down the steps toward her car, then glanced back over her shoulder. "I'll see you at the farm for the council fundraiser in a few days."

He nodded. "See you there."

He watched as she got in her car and backed out of his drive before taking in a deep breath. Why did just seeing her and knowing she wanted to check on him stir up so many emotions? He couldn't explain it and wasn't going to try to decipher his own headspace now. His family was inside, no doubt wondering if Violet was coming in.

Dax raked a hand over the back of his neck and prayed for patience and strength to get through this time with his family and keep up with this little fib.

He had to assume he and Violet were keeping this all superficial and relaxed. They hadn't really gone over the logistics, but he figured they'd be in agreement that their families only needed to believe they were dating and no dates had to actually happen.

And as far as Violet's past went, he had no idea what had happened to make her seem standoffish and a bit reserved. And quite honestly, her history wasn't his business. Of course he couldn't tell his family that part.

The moment he stepped back into the kitchen, all eyes were on him.

"So you met Rachel," Dax started. "And got Violet to pick out some flowers for the porch."

Both his mother and his sister let out a little "aww" and shot each other a glance. Great. Not what he needed. Them falling deeper in with Violet was not part of this setup.

His father placed the glasses he was holding on the counter and shrugged. "It was a productive trip. I look forward to meeting the rest of the family at the council fundraiser."

Was it too late for him to bail? People would still donate to the town council for all they did even if the new sheriff wasn't there, right? Maybe he could feign being sick. He'd already faked a relationship. What was one more thing?

Goodness, he was falling down the rabbit hole of lies and that was not the man he wanted to be, nor was that the man he'd been raised to be. He was stronger than this and he would remain firm in his faith and his morals—as much as he could.

"I'm sure the whole town will be there. You'll be able to meet a good many people." Dax grabbed a plate and started filling it up as he moved around the island toward the stove. "This looks amazing. Thanks for invading my house and for painting my spare bedroom."

"No problem." His sister practically sang. "I was thinking of a soft yellow for the living room. Just a hint of color, you know? So when the sun shines through that big picture window it's just enough so it's not plain."

There with the color yellow again. Maybe June was here in spirit helping him settle in.

"Can you keep your decorating to a minimum?" he asked, scooping up gooey potatoes. "I don't think every room needs paint. Do you?"

"Most of them."

"Just let her go, son," his father murmured, stepping in beside him. "That will take up the most time. Otherwise she'll try to find new furniture and the place will be filled with things you don't like."

"I can hear you guys, you know," Clara called out.

"Then don't do anything else beyond painting my living room. And no crazy color." Dax turned back around with his plate and met her gaze. "I mean it. No cutesy sayings on my walls or big floral arrangements on the tables. I have zero reasons for throw pillows. You paint, I'll decorate. Got it?"

She snapped her heels together and gave a mock salute. "Yes, sir!"

"Always the smarty-pants," he muttered.

"Go on into the dining room," his mother told him. "I got that set up earlier. Not sure if that's how you want things, but it'll do for now."

Dax jerked around to face her. "I didn't have a dining room table."

"You do now," she told him with a smile. "But if you don't like it, I can return it. I made sure before I purchased it. I know you want to do everything yourself, I just wanted to help a little."

He glanced to his father, who merely shrugged once again. These strong-willed women were ruling the house. On one hand he was glad he didn't have to think about much, but on the other he wanted to make this place his. Still, he shouldn't complain when they were only doing this out of love. He'd be thankful they loved him enough to put forth all this effort. In less than two weeks they'd be gone and back in Oregon and he'd miss them like crazy. He hadn't realized just how much he missed their presence until they showed up on his doorstep like a welcome wagon.

The moment Dax stepped into the dining room, he was actually surprised that the dark wood table and sturdy chairs and bench were exactly something he would've chosen himself. The tall rounded-back chairs at the ends of the table had armrests and were different from the other chairs, while one side of the table had a nice, long bench. He almost chuckled because he wasn't sure how many people his mother thought he'd be entertaining, but this setup could easily seat twelve.

She'd even put a navy blue table runner with a thick, fat glass jar and a white candle in the middle. Something decorative but not over-the-top feminine. There was already so much love in his new house, but he still had that unsettled feeling deep in his gut from the deceit he'd caused right off the bat. He couldn't relax around his family for the lies that rested between them, and he couldn't relax around Violet for dragging her into this, not to mention the fact he found her far too attractive and adorable. The combination made for one gigantic ball of unwanted nerves.

"It's just a little housewarming gift."

Dax set his plate on the table as his mother came in behind him.

"I love it." Dax moved around the table and pulled her into an embrace. "But I thought that's what the plants on the porch were for."

Her slender arms wrapped around his waist as she patted his back. "Oh, that's just because your porch needed some life. I wanted to get you something nice for your first new place. This is a big step for you and I'm so proud."

When she sniffed, his heart clenched. He eased back slightly, curling his fingers around her delicate shoulders.

"Don't cry, Mom. I'm fine," he assured her. "Junie would want this for me and I feel at peace with my decision to come here."

Well, he had been at peace up until the moment when he decided putting his family's minds at ease trumped his own moral compass.

"I know." She nodded with another sniff. "I just miss you."

"Oh, great," Clara grunted as she came in. "What did you say to make her cry?"

"It's Mom. I don't have to say anything. She cries when she's happy and sad."

His mom swatted his chest. Even though he towered over her, she still demanded respect and he certainly did respect her. There was no other woman he adored more.

"You just wait until you two are parents," she scolded. "It takes its toll on your mental state. Now, I'm going to go compose myself and get my dinner and I'll be right back."

"I already got your plate."

Dax's father came in carrying two full plates. "You go get yourself ready and grab our drinks. I'll wait to say the blessing."

That void in Dax's heart was always there, but there were certain times it made itself known. Like now. When his parents were there for each other, having one another to lean on without even asking. That was the type of love he and his Junie had had. That was the type of love he thought he'd have for another fifty-plus years. But a distracted driver had robbed Dax and June of that chance of happiness and a family.

Of course, he was so happy for his parents to have their decades of love. Dax just wished he could add himself to that group. One day, who knows? Maybe God had more plans for him, but for now Dax just wanted to get rooted in his new town and start this new life and carry on the Adams name and reputation in Rosewood Valley. That's all he wanted to concentrate on right now. Everything else would have to wait or come in God's time.

Chapter Eight

"Don't you think the drinks should go on the other side?" Violet asked.

Rachel shook her head. "Why would we do that? They've always been here. And why are you so fidgety?"

"Because her guy should be here any minute," Jenn stated as she came by with a homemade coconut cream pie for the dessert table.

Violet nearly said "He's not my guy" but thankfully caught herself before the words could slip out. And maybe that was why she was nervous, but no way would she admit such a thing.

"I'm just not usually so hands-on with these events," she replied, going with the truth. "I usually help when and where I can and not so much from start to finish. I'm just stressed lately."

Again, very much the truth. With her crazy schedule leading up to her own event, she'd barely been able to put in the dedicated hours for this one. Because this was Four Sisters' biggest farm-to-table dinner they'd ever done, Violet didn't want to leave them without that extra set of hands for the setup and when it was time to tear everything down. She would certainly crash in her bed tonight. She already couldn't wait to snuggle beneath her nice thick comforter.

"We could have handled this, you know." Rachel laid her hand on Violet's arm and gave it a gentle squeeze. "I know the timing of this isn't ideal, but Dax set the date and we had an opening so we locked it in."

"Of course," Violet agreed. "As you should. The farm and family come first, which is why I'm here running on caffeine and five hours of sleep each night for the past couple of weeks. All will be good after my fundraiser. No worries."

After the fundraiser and after the guilt and anxiety of being a pretend girlfriend were gone.

"Granted you all weren't dating then so there was no way of knowing everything would collide into one perfect storm," Rachel added.

Perfect storm? That description might be the best one yet to describe this last-minute ruse.

"Well, we'll all pitch in where we're needed for Pets in the Park," Jenn chimed in as she breezed by once again.

"I can't wait to pick out a new pet!" Paisley exclaimed as she followed behind Jenn.

Paisley had been put to work and was running back and forth just like the rest of them.

She might only be eight years old, but she was mature and had been through quite a bit in that short time, forcing her to grow up far beyond her years.

"I think we should talk to Luke before we start planning on another pet," Jenn warned. "We already have Cookie."

"How about we get through today first," Violet suggested, offering a smile. "We've got a lot of important people from the town coming and Dax's family is here. I know this has to be somewhat stressful for him."

That was just an assumption based on how she'd feel if she were in his shoes. She honestly had no clue if he was nervous or not.

Rachel dropped her hand and started to say something else, but their parents stepped through the wide-open barn doors. Will and Sarah Spencer didn't always attend the farm events together, but when the entire town of Rosewood Valley had RSVP'd they'd attend, it was no surprise they'd want to be part of the evening's festivities. And her parents looked so sweet, Violet couldn't help but smile. She adored them and their tight bond. They'd dressed up so nice for the evening, exchanging their usual work and farm attire for something semiformal. Her mother was wearing a long blue dress that was draped and gathered beautifully at the waist with a match-

ing silk flower. Her father had black dress pants
and a matching jacket, no doubt with his signature red suspenders hidden beneath. Everyone
in town knew Will Spencer by those red straps.

"Oh, girls, this looks absolutely stunning!"
Her mother stopped just inside the doorway and
clasped her hands together as her eyes surveyed
the decorated area. "Just when I think you all
can't outdo yourselves, you go and do just that.
This is perfect."

She moved to the closest guest table and carefully ran a finger over one of the white birch
vines popping up from the table arrangements.
As she continued to murmur her praise, their father headed straight to the sweets.

"Mom told him to cut back after his last doctor appointment," Rachel whispered. "Apparently his A1C is inching up there."

Violet knew how much her father loved his
baked goods and she wasn't about to stand in
his way. She had enough on her own plate without getting in the middle of her parents and their
doctor's orders.

"He probably thinks she won't notice." Violet laughed. "Especially once this place gets full
and so much is going on."

"Oh, yeah. He'll definitely be sneaking a piece
of banana cream pie to the back." Rachel nodded
in agreement, then glanced around. Her brows

drew together as she pursed her lips. "Wonder where Erin is? She should've been here by now."

"Maybe she couldn't get her hair fixed or couldn't find something to wear," Vi suggested. "She'll be here."

Will Spencer came up and wrapped an arm around Vi and Rachel, dropping a kiss on each of their heads.

"Beautiful and talented," he stated. Jenn crossed from the dessert table and wiped her hand on the apron she wore over her cream-colored maxi dress. Will offered her a hug, too. "I'd expect nothing less from my gene pool. Now, where is my fourth daughter?"

"I haven't heard from her, either," Jenn said. "Maybe we should text her and see where she is."

"I'll do it," their mom piped up from behind. "But I'm calling. Too much texting and not enough calling these days. This generation— I tell ya."

Still mumbling about too much screen time, she pulled her cell from the pocket of her long blue skirt and tapped the screen as she turned away. Violet wasn't too concerned about her missing sister. Erin was just as reliable as the rest of them. They'd been brought up with manners, and that included punctuality and dependability. Erin wasn't one to be fussy, either. So who knew what was holding her up. If she didn't like her hair, she'd put it in a classy low bun and head out the door.

"So, what else needs done?" Violet asked.

"I think that's it." Rachel stepped away from their father and moved toward the far corner. "Just let me get this music going so it's not dead air when people arrive and we'll be good to go. Dax and his family will probably be here first."

Yes. That was precisely what worried Violet. Dax's family and her family in here alone for any period of time would only be a recipe for disaster. Or maybe they'd all just start chatting and ignore her and Dax altogether. Wouldn't that be nice?

"She's on her way."

Violet's father turned to face her mother. She had a smile on her face as she eased her phone back into her pocket.

"Her car wouldn't start, but she got it going," her mother explained. "I've told her over and over to get something else, but that girl is stubborn just like her father."

"How did I get pulled into this?" her dad asked. "I offered to help her look for a car, but she wants to keep saving her money."

Her mother sighed. "Well, she's going to be going by horse and buggy or bicycle if she won't let go of those purse strings."

Violet tuned out her parents as they went back and forth over Erin's predicament. As an elementary school teacher, Erin didn't have a huge income but enough for a single person. Still, she was smart about her purchases, but this car problem might warrant a shopping trip. With summer here, she needed to get her vehicle taken care of before school started back up and she had even more problems with trying to get to work on time.

Violet had her own issues that worried her without trying to mentally fix Erin's troubles. Vi fixed her eyes on the doorway as she waited on Dax and his family to arrive. She smoothed a hand down her dress and wondered if curling her hair had been too much. Maybe she should've left it straight. She rarely even wore it down let alone took a hot tool to it. She should've done a clear gloss and not the pink. She'd definitely done too much.

Why was her stomach tied in knots? This was so silly and her nerves spiraled as if Dax was picking her up for a high school dance. How ridiculous was that? She wasn't *actually* dating him and she certainly wasn't worried about impressing him. They were merely doing each other a favor—that was all.

So why had she saved that image of him and Colt to her phone? She could have left that image sitting right there in their text messages but no. She'd wanted that adorable picture all for herself. Maybe she was getting too wrapped up in this.

Music filtered through the hidden sound system they'd had installed—instrumental country. Violet assumed that's what Dax had asked for. Or Rachel had chosen something. She was very good at working with each client on their needs and the initial questionnaire when booking the event space was quite extensive.

The crunching sound of tires over gravel had her heart picking up. Was this Dax or Erin? Violet didn't want to look too anxious so she moved toward the entryway just to greet the guests in case it was Dax and his family. That's what she should do, right?

Before she could make it to the door, Dax and his family appeared. Violet stilled. She beheld the entire foursome against the gorgeous backdrop of a soft glow from the sun descending behind the mountains of Northern California. The entire clan looked perfect for a night to represent the sheriff.

But it was the sheriff himself who captured her attention. Of course he had on his uniform, but it was that intense stare he aimed directly at her that knotted her stomach.

"Oh, you're here." Violet's mother maneuvered around her and greeted them, just like

Violet should be doing if she hadn't somehow found herself frozen in place. The trance she and Dax seemed to be in shocked her, and an unexpected rush of emotions left her overwhelmed and confused.

"I'm Sarah Spencer," her mother greeted as she opened her arms to hug each member of Dax's family. "Welcome to Four Sisters."

"I'm Kay and this is my husband, Mike." Dax's mom did introductions as she smiled and pointed. "And this is Dax's twin sister, Clara."

"This is so wonderful to have you all in town for this occasion," her mother went on.

She caught her sister moving toward the group. "I'm Rachel."

Her father came up as well as Jenn, greeting their guests and shaking hands. Vi found herself taking one step forward, then another, until she stood before Dax. His eyes still remained on her and she wasn't sure if she wanted to know what he was thinking. Did he think she looked pretty or was he wishing he could get out of this whole mess?

"I'm so glad our families can meet before everyone gets here," Kay stated. "I just adore Violet and can't wait to get to know her more. I haven't seen my son this happy in a long time."

Violet watched a flurry of expressions flood over Dax's face. She couldn't quite identify all his emotions, but she definitely saw heartache and maybe a hint of embarrassment.

"Can I talk to you?" she murmured, then nodded toward the exterior.

She glanced at the gathering of family members who had all turned their eyes in their direction. Her stomach twisted again and she found herself taking a step toward Dax. She couldn't explain why, but she needed to be closer to him. Maybe because he was the only one who understood the inner turmoil. She'd seen that same discomfort in his eyes that she was feeling now. All she knew was she needed to get away and she had a feeling he did, too.

"Is everything okay?" her mother asked.

Violet kept her smile firmly in place. "Everything is fine. Just need to steal Dax for a quick moment before the party starts."

Without hesitation or another passing thought, she grabbed his hand, led him out of the barn and didn't stop until she was around the side of the building.

"Care to tell me why you're dragging me?" he asked with a chuckle.

Violet whipped around as Dax's blue eyes darted down to their joined hands. She immediately released him, then hated how she missed the innocent touch.

"Sorry." She rubbed the tips of her fingers together, wondering why they tingled. "I needed an escape so I opted to take you with me."

His smile faltered as his steady gaze settled on her once again. She truly had no clue what was going through his mind, but she wished he'd say something or stop staring because this awkward tension was not helping to settle her nerves.

He hadn't expected this. And by "this" he meant a whole new side to Violet that he'd never seen. He'd seen the town vet side with her scrubs and messy ponytail. He'd seen the friendly neighbor side, void of any makeup, but the woman who'd greeted him earlier had stolen his breath and rendered him speechless.

Whatever Violet had done to herself had taken her from cute girl next door to stunning, and he had no idea what to do other than stare like some teen with a crush on the popular cheerleader. The yellow dress gave her skin a golden glow and she'd put on a soft pink gloss that wasn't overly done, but just enough to make her smile even more striking. Her hair was down, which he'd never seen, and flowing down her back in soft waves.

There was no denying each of the four Spencer sisters had a beauty all their own. But Violet had that wholesome innocence about her that intrigued him because he knew she was also so strong and bold. Tonight, her look was bolder than he'd ever seen.

"Is something wrong?" she asked, glancing down at her dress, then smoothing her hair back.

Goodness. Now all his ridiculous staring had her feeling self-conscious and fidgety. She definitely had no reason whatsoever to have any doubts about her appearance—not tonight or any other time.

"No, no," he assured her. "Nothing is wrong."

At least nothing with her. If anything was wrong, it was only in his own mind. Should he be this attracted to her? Should he be this attracted to any woman when he'd loved his Junie so much? His therapist and his pastor had told him that moving on was a natural part of life and that it would happen one day, that he shouldn't feel guilty when he started having feelings for another woman. Had that time come? Was Violet that woman or was he just confused?

Yesterday when she'd stopped by his house, he hadn't been able to put a finger on how he'd felt, but now he knew. Rescued. That was the word that seemed to embody Violet and her actions toward him, which only left him more confused.

One thing was clear: she looked amazing tonight. If they couldn't be completely honest with everyone else, they had to be one hundred percent honest with each other.

"You look beautiful." He took a step forward, closing the small gap between them. "I was just taken off guard, to be honest. I'm not used to seeing you in a dress."

"Oh. Well." Violet blinked. "Yeah. It's not often. Church is usually the only time I'm in a dress unless I have a wedding or special occasion to attend."

Once again he found himself staring at her as if seeing her for the very first time. She'd also done something to her wide green eyes. Something to make them even more intense, and he found himself drowning in them. He was slipping here, on this unfamiliar slope he'd created. He had nobody to blame but himself, but right now he couldn't even form a coherent thought. He was just trying to figure out how to make it through this evening without staring across the room at Violet. Even if they were dating for real, that wouldn't look too professional. If the highest power in the town couldn't keep his eyes off his girlfriend—well, that would be pretty pathetic and adolescent behavior.

"I guess I should dress up more," she went on. "I just don't really have a reason and the animals never care what I'm wearing." She laughed a little self-consciously.

"No." He shook his head and leaned in just a fraction more. "Don't change a thing."

The wind kicked up, sending strands of her honey hair dancing around her shoulders. She eased the pieces away, trying to tuck them behind her ears, but her bright green eyes never wavered from his.

"Don't you go to the same church I do?" she asked. "How have I never seen you there?"

He suppressed a grin at her anxious energy and obvious nervous chatter. He wasn't feeling too calm himself and didn't know whether to chalk it up to the fact their families were all mingling together or that he had some unwanted, unexplained emotions curling through his body.

"We go to different services," he stated. "I'm the first service."

"Oh, well. I'm the second," she explained. "Then we're both in jobs that call us out at the most random times, too, so sometimes I miss as I'm sure you do."

He nodded, still watching her golden hair move about. He fisted his hands at his sides to keep from reaching out. He had no right. They weren't dating or even friends—or maybe they were. He honestly didn't know what they were, but he knew each time he was around her he only became more confused on what he thought he should want and what he thought he was actually ready for.

Maybe he *was* ready to date again—for real.

The thought had hope flaring in him—but it also terrified him. How could he ever give his heart to someone so fully like he had to June? What if it broke again?

"Do you think they're still in there talking about us?" Violet asked, pulling him from his thoughts.

"I have no doubt."

His sister was likely quizzing her sisters about the farm and the lifestyle here in Rosewood Valley. And if he knew Clara, she was also asking all about Violet. His twin would want to know everything about the woman Dax was seeing.

He absolutely hated lying to them, yet he knew they would leave here at the end of their visit with peace in their hearts that only this avenue could provide. Once they were back home and settled in, he would inform them that he and Violet realized they were better as friends. And he truly believed they could be friends after all was said and done. He wanted her in his life— Violet wasn't the kind of person you could let into your life and then let go of easily.

"You do look really nice," he said. "It doesn't matter if you have on your scrubs or a dress, a man would notice. He'd be foolish not to."

Her eyes widened at the compliment, and he noticed again how green they were. Unable to resist any longer, Dax reached out and eased her hair behind her ear. His fingertips feathered along her jawline and it was Violet who took a step closer this time until the toes of their shoes tapped.

What was it with this invisible pull toward her? He didn't suddenly find her more interesting and attractive because she'd dressed up. No, this was just another layer he found intriguing. Maybe it was the way she'd looked at him when he'd first arrived. Or the way she'd taken his hand, assuming he needed a moment's break. Dax couldn't quite put his finger on how Violet managed to keep him in some inner circle around her.

But this was just pretend, right?

Yet who was around to see the act? Not a soul. He had no idea how long they'd been looking at each other, but he was aware of her soft skin beneath his fingertips.

"Hey, guys."

Dax dropped his hand at the unfamiliar voice. He turned to see Violet's other sister, Erin, waving as she dashed toward the barn from her car. She breezed past, clearly paying no mind to them having a moment because to her, Dax and Vi were dating. Nothing to see here.

But the moment of reprieve had him rethinking what he'd been about to do. He'd nearly kissed her. As that sunk in, something in him shifted, and he didn't know when or where or how to get back on track to where he needed to be for his sanity. He was still settling into a new town, a new role. If he even thought he was ready to try to date again, he needed to take things slow. Rushing things with a woman he'd met a few days ago would be disastrous.

"Sorry," he told her once they were alone again. He stepped back.

She stared at him another second before her gaze darted away. The radiance from the sun cast a warm glow over her upturned face and he had to take another step back. He had to remove himself both emotionally and physically. Until he had a solid foundation, he couldn't bring anyone else into his world.

And taking a huge step like a relationship was something he had to pray about above all else. Trying to enter into anything with Violet sounded like a bad idea. But were they even authentic? Or was he just caught up in the moment?

"You were looking at me like…" came her soft voice.

"Like what?" he finally asked when she said nothing.

Her eyes turned back to focus on his. "Like you wanted to kiss me."

His heart clenched and words failed.

"But that's ridiculous, isn't it?" she added with

a small smile that didn't quite reach her eyes. "We're not attracted to each other. We don't even know each other, right?"

"Right." He swallowed the lump in his throat as he nodded in agreement. "It's ridiculous. You just threw me off."

He sighed and extended his arm for her. "Should I escort you back inside? Our families will wonder if we left."

Violet's smile did nothing to squelch his growing attraction. He had to keep his thoughts and feelings to himself. There was no way he could tell her or act on them. Touching her cheek had been a serious mistake because the tips of his fingers still tingled from that harmless graze.

He was in some serious trouble here.

Violet slid her hand in the crook of his arm and he led the way back toward the barn. Thankfully another car turned into the lot, breaking the rest of whatever trance he'd been in. With the party starting, he had to be in full community service member mode. He needed the distraction of talking with other people to take his mind off his jumbled thoughts about Violet.

He placed his hand gently over hers as he escorted her back inside. Once again, that connection turned something inside him that hadn't clicked in so long. Dax couldn't trust what he was feeling.

"You two are back." Rachel's eyes darted between them and her smile widened. "We were starting to take bets on if you were going to join us."

"I was hoping you guys were skipping out for a romantic evening," Clara admitted, wiggling her brows.

Violet's grip on his arm tightened just slightly, but enough to know their words affected her. He gave a side glance and wasn't a bit surprised to still see her smiling. That was who she was. She knew their families would be excited for them, and her need to put others ahead of herself spoke volumes on her character—which didn't help his fascination one bit.

He had a surprise for her later and he only hoped she appreciated what he'd done. His idea had been inspired by her, but he'd taken her generosity and run with it.

"I know my obligations," he stated, keeping his hold on Violet's hand, partly for show, but if he was honest, mostly because he just wanted to. "We just needed a quick private chat."

"Don't they look great together." His mother came up to stand next to Rachel. "They complement each other so well. I'm so happy you can do this event together as a unit."

A unit?

Violet tensed beside him, mimicking his own

internal thoughts. But they were doing it. They were actually pulling this whole relationship thing off. This public event was their biggest audience, likely their only audience, during their two-week run at this.

"Yes," Rachel agreed. "Now that the town's most eligible bachelor is taken, and by a woman the town already loves and adores, this evening's fundraiser is the perfect time for everyone to see them together."

Violet started forward, but he gently held her in place as he spoke up on both of their behalf.

"This isn't a party about Violet and me," he informed them. "This is to raise necessary funds to keep Rosewood Valley running properly and partly as an appreciation and thank-you from me for everyone taking a chance on an outsider."

"Oh, please," his mother scoffed. "You might not have grown up here, but your father's ancestors founded this town and nobody has deeper roots here than you do. You were the perfect candidate and the council saw that."

There had only been one other applicant for the position and when he didn't get the promotion, he'd moved away.

Erin made her way over and this was the first time Dax had seen this sister up close. She had a sweet smile and pretty eyes just like the other three, but none captured his attention the way Violet managed to.

"Hi. I'm Erin." She held out her hand in greeting. "We haven't formally met but since you're dating my sister it's probably time."

He shook her hand before placing his right back on Violet's. "Pleasure to meet you."

Erin's attention turned to Violet. "I'm sorry I was late and couldn't finish with the final touches. My car keeps acting up."

"No worries. We got it," Violet assured her. "But you really should consider upgrading. You've had that thing since college."

Erin shrugged. "We'll see. I don't want to give up on it just yet and I'm trying to save for something important."

A couple of guests appeared in the doorway and Dax released Violet as they all stepped out of the way. She moved even farther away and made her way toward her parents, then began talking and pointing toward the food tables. He should've known she'd do something to keep busy. She probably needed a minute to herself, too.

Ironically enough, the whole point of this joint venture was for show, but he understood her need for privacy and could one hundred percent respect her wishes. He had his own duties to attend to and needed the distraction.

Violet caught his gaze once more and stilled for just a second before turning her focus back to her father. Yet it was long enough for Dax to wonder what she'd been thinking. He forced his eyes away from her and questioned why he'd ever thought that a deal with Violet Spencer would be the solution to all his problems. Instead, it had only created more.

Chapter Nine

Tender touches, long glances, sweet compliments—all that had to go. She couldn't find him adorable or charming.

Violet moved about the venue chatting with guests while subtly checking the trays of food to see when and if things needed to be refilled. The party had been in full swing for a good hour and so far she hadn't had to pair up with Dax for a united showing like their sisters seemed to think was a good plan.

But she'd felt his eyes on her most of the evening. She'd turn and there he'd be, looking at her. He didn't even try to hide it, either. The nerve of that man keeping her off-kilter. She wanted her kilter on, thank you very much.

"Violet, you and your family have outdone yourselves as always."

Vi smiled as Sharma Townsend, head of the town council, eased around one of the tables toward her.

"Thank you, Sharma," Violet replied. "We're happy to have such a great turnout."

"Oh, you know the town wouldn't miss a good party, especially at Four Sisters." Sharma leaned in and whispered, "Especially now that we know our new sheriff is so smitten with one of those sisters."

Violet forced her smile to remain firmly in place.

"I'm not so sure about smitten." Violet laughed, more from nerves than anything else. "Have you tried the peach tartlets? My mother tried a new recipe just for this event and I think they're going to be a new item on the catering menu."

Thankfully, Sharma moved the conversation on to an upcoming event she would be hosting for a ladies' guild and mentioned she wanted those exact desserts. Violet didn't care what she wanted for desserts; she'd make it happen, so long as the conversation didn't steer back to Dax.

"I'm sure Rachel and my mother will take great care of you and your party," Violet assured her. "Rachel's the guru for organizing all the things and making these events run so smoothly, and you know how Mom is in the kitchen. The rest of us are just fillers showing up where we're needed."

"Oh, I know this is a team effort," Sharma stated, adjusting her rhinestone glasses. "I just love how the town is growing with new things like this. Our farmers market is starting back up soon and your mama's goods are always a hit."

Sarah Spencer did have the best produce, canned goods and baked goods in the county. When they were younger, Violet and her sisters always spent all winter preparing for the start of market season. They still helped when they could but as they'd grown and gotten their own careers and lives, making time to all get together had become more and more difficult. Which was just another reason why Violet loved having this venue so much. They could all work together to not only help supplement income for the farm, but also spend precious quality time like they used to.

"How's Pets in the Park coming along?" Sharma asked. "That's always another fun event for the town."

"Coming right along." Whether Violet was ready or not. "We have a few new things added this year and even more pets that need adopting, so hopefully we have good weather and a great turnout."

"Well, I've seen signs in all the businesses and everyone is sharing the social media posts. I'm sure it will be another huge success for you."

Violet didn't want the success for herself—she wanted it for the animals who deserved loving homes. But before she could say anything of the sort, Sharma waved her hand and smiled at someone over Violet's shoulder.

"There's your guy now," Sharma whispered. "I'll excuse myself so you two can talk."

Her guy. Everyone kept saying that. She hadn't had a *guy* since Chance deceived her and she had had to make the difficult decision to end their relationship. Soon she and Dax would go their separate ways. Except she didn't know if she could forget that delicate touch or the way he'd stared into her eyes like he had a direct line of sight into her soul. She didn't want to be so cliché as to fall for a man in uniform—and she wasn't. She certainly wasn't falling for Dax Adams. He irked her, or he used to. She really couldn't recall when she stopped being so annoyed with him and when she'd started to care about him. But she did. She wanted good things for him, like that new beginning he was after. She'd become much too interested in his life.

"Vi."

That low tone of his sent a shiver through her and she realized he'd never called her by her nickname. That was something she'd have to address. She needed to keep this more formal so she didn't lose herself or worse—start liking him on a whole other level that wouldn't do either of them any good.

Violet turned and pasted a smile. "Yes?"

He leaned in. "Your sister Erin could use some rescuing. I believe Garnet Trulane has her cornered. They were just chatting and then someone named Joe was brought up and your sister froze in place and looked like she wanted to flee all at the same time."

Violet's gaze darted around the wide area looking for Erin. Of course her sister wanted to escape *that* conversation. Joe Trulane was the only man she'd ever loved. He'd left town long ago to pursue his dream of becoming a missionary, and Garnet, his grandmother, still believed the two belonged together. But the relationship between Erin and Garnet had been strained since Joe's departure, so who knew what was happening over there.

"Thanks for the heads-up," Violet told him. "I'll go find her."

Dax pointed toward the front of the barn. "That way."

She nodded and made her way toward the situation. While she worried for her sister's well-being, it was not lost on her how Dax had noticed the problem and immediately come to her for help. He was trained to read people, but the fact he'd picked up on someone's internal conflict really impressed Violet. She shook the thought from her head. They were still lying, and she still didn't like it one bit.

"Isn't that exciting?" Garnet's words filtered to Violet as she approached.

"Joe hasn't been back in years and he'll be here in just a few months. I can hardly stand it," she went on. "I just know he'll want to see you again."

Violet stepped right next to her sister and placed a hand on her back. "Good evening, Garnet. You are looking lovely in that peach dress."

"Oh, why thank you, dear." The elderly lady smiled as she smoothed a hand down the floral material. "I bought this for a wedding shower that I never attended because I simply couldn't bring myself to go to something I didn't agree with. The wedding never happened, so I feel my instincts were spot-on with that one."

Violet continued to smile as her sister's tense body leaned toward her.

"I was just telling Erin how my Joe will be back from Africa at the end of August, and I cannot wait," Garnet went on. "They'll have to do dinner so they can catch up."

Oh, no. That would just be a disaster waiting to happen.

"Garnet—"

"If you'll excuse us." Violet cut off her sister and took her by the hand to ease her away. "I need some help in the kitchen getting more food out. I'm so thrilled you're getting your grandson home."

Once Violet and Erin were away, Vi let go of her sister's hand but kept walking toward the kitchen. Finally behind the privacy of the closed door, Violet faced her sister, who appeared to be taking deep breaths.

"You good?" Violet asked.

Erin leaned against the counter and rested her hands on either side of her body. She nodded and tipped her head back.

"How did you know I needed saving?" she asked.

"Dax told me."

Her brows rose. "I didn't even see him go by," she admitted. "I still love Garnet, but we've barely spoken since Joe left and she just swooped in with this bombshell. The thought of facing him again…"

Violet had no clue how her sister still felt about Joe, but clearly there were unresolved feelings. The only thing Violet knew was that when Joe left, Erin had shut down for a long time. She had closed herself off from everyone and barely smiled. It had taken a long time to see her sister come around and she really didn't want Erin to fall back into that dark place again.

"You're a stronger woman now," Violet told

her. "You have a career you love, you're busy with our venue and you've been working toward fostering a child. You have a whole new life since Joe left and I'm sure he does, too."

Erin nodded. "I know. Just the thought of him coming back makes me wonder if seeing him will put me right back into that time and place and mindset of the girl he left behind."

The kitchen door opened and Jenn stepped through, then stopped short when she spotted them.

"Oh, sorry." Her eyes darted between them. "Wait. What's wrong?"

"Joe is coming back to town," Violet explained.

"Joe?" Jenn repeated. "As in… *Joe*?"

Erin nodded. "*The* Joe."

Jenn moved to the far counter and came back with a bite-size cheesecake with a single raspberry on top. She held it out to Erin.

"Here," she offered. "You need some carbs while you process this."

Violet swatted her hand. "We're supposed to be telling her how she'll be stronger seeing him now than she was before because she's grown since then."

Jenn jerked slightly. "Oh, yeah. That, too. But you still could use some carbs."

Violet rolled her eyes. "Everything will be fine, Erin. I promise."

Erin took the sweet treat, plucked the berry off the top and dropped it into her mouth. "That's easy for you all to say. All of my sisters have a guy now. You're all smiling and happy and getting settled. I go home to an empty house and spend my nights grading papers and hoping my car will start the next morning. It's the most boring life, but I'm not complaining. I'm just... Okay, maybe I was complaining. But you guys seem on a different level of contentment, and I'm not sure I'll ever have that."

There went that guilt sliding through Violet once again. Just when she seemed to forget, it came right back to the front. She didn't know what to say without laying on another lie and she simply couldn't do that, not when Erin was clearly hurting.

"God has a plan for you, too," Jenn reminded Erin. "You know Mom and Dad have always said it's not our timing, but His."

Erin finished the cheesecake in two quick bites and shrugged. "Yeah, I know. That news just threw me off. I promise not to sulk and feel sorry for myself. I just needed a second."

"Take all the time you need," Jenn told her. "We've got it covered. I actually just came in to grab more drink napkins. The new punch recipe I suggested is a hit."

Violet gave Erin a quick hug and excused herself. She pushed through the swinging door and took a moment for herself as she surveyed the area. The soft country tunes continued to play as familiar faces she'd known her entire life moved about. Folks laughed and chatted. Some were coming back for more finger foods and desserts. There was something so special about what she and her family had created here. Bringing people together in fellowship or to celebrate a special occasion brought a smile to her face, even though she might be facing internal turmoil.

"I haven't seen her that upset in so long."

Rachel stepped up beside her and Violet nodded in agreement. "At least she has a heads-up and Joe didn't just show up back in town with no warning."

"True," Rachel said. "She'll be just fine." She faced Violet, a smile forming on her lips. "But let's talk about how your guy can't keep his eyes off you."

"What?" Violet jerked her attention to her older sister.

Rachel's smile spread wide. "Clearly, when the sheriff fell, he fell hard."

Oh, no, he most certainly did not. There was no falling, except at the end of this two weeks they'd be falling out of this entire ordeal and right back into their normal lives.

"I'm not so sure about that," Violet finally replied. "We just started this thing so let's not get carried away."

All the truth, which she had to cling as close to as possible.

"Looks like the sheriff needs you," came Jenn's voice.

Her sister gestured toward the stage on the opposite side of the barn where Dax stood and was motioning for Violet to join him. What on earth was he doing? There was absolutely no reason for her to be part of the actual festivities and he'd given her no indication that she'd be front and center for anything of the sort.

As all eyes in the place turned and looked in her direction, Violet forced a grin as her belly constricted into a tight ball of knots. She wound her way through the guests and the tables and headed toward the stage. Dax extended his hand to assist her up the two small steps, and as she laid her palm over his, he merely offered a smile that seemed both sly and endearing.

What was she getting herself into? Or more to the point, what was *he* getting her into?

Chapter Ten

Maybe he was going over-the-top, but his parents and Clara were standing in the front, and he'd sought Violet out without even thinking. For reasons he couldn't explain, he felt more comfortable with her, especially in this setting.

He hated speaking in front of people like this. Considering he was the one who'd decided to host this event, he felt he should say a few words of thanks. But having Violet next to him made him less nervous.

Dax released her hand as soon as she stood at his side. She stared at him with a whole host of silent questions in those expressive eyes of hers. There wasn't a doubt in his mind they'd be having a chat later.

Dax scanned the large crowd, recognizing many faces, but seeing some he was still getting to know. "Thank you all for coming out this evening and supporting not only me, but also Four Sisters," he said into the mic. "I know I'm new to Rosewood Valley, but my roots were planted

firmly decades ago when my great-great-grandfather became your first sheriff. Family is very
important to me, as I'm sure it is to all of you. I
hope to serve as your sheriff for years to come,
and I'm so happy to start my new chapter here."
He looked out into a sea of smiling faces, then
continued, "I just want to thank you for welcoming me into your town. I have instantly felt at
home and I want to especially thank Violet and
her family for making this evening so perfect
with the venue, the food and the music. Please,
consider bidding on some of the amazing auc-
tion items along the back wall or you can make
any donation that will go directly into our city
fund to help with keeping our beautiful town
running. We couldn't do this without you all."

The crowd erupted into applause and Violet continued to hold her smile firmly in place
as she glanced at him. Others might see her as
sweet and supportive, but he was pretty sure she
wanted to be anywhere else other than this stage.
Yet here she stood by his side because he'd asked
her to. Or rather, he'd forced her hand and she
was too polite to say no.

Violet stepped up and gestured for the mic,
which he passed to her. "I would also like to
thank everyone for coming out," she said once
the applause died down. "My family cannot
thank you all enough for the support. I can't

think of a better way to rally behind our new sheriff than a town gathering. And I'd like to add a shameless plug for my Pets in the Park fundraiser coming up in less than two weeks. I hope to see you all there. And please, eat more cheesecake and take some home." The crowd tittered at her words—she was so charming.

"One more thing," Dax stated, holding up his hand to keep the audience's attention. "We will be taking up separate donations for a summer program for underprivileged children in the area. We want to make sure these kids have something to do in the summer other than getting into trouble or stuck in a situation that isn't safe. Any donations can be dropped off at the sheriff's department or given to me or any of my deputies directly. This is a program I hope to grow from year to year, and I know I can count on this town for support. Thank you all so much."

Violet's slight gasp couldn't be heard over the additional applause of the crowd, but when he cast her a sideways glance, he couldn't suppress his smile. He'd actually caught her off guard. And while he didn't know her well, he was pretty certain he'd made her happy.

That pleased him in a way he hadn't expected. A warmth overwhelmed him and once the shock settled from her face, her shoulders relaxed and her lips turned up into a soft smile. She mouthed a simple thank-you and he nodded his response. He'd seen a need and the timing of this event was the best way he knew to spread the word in a quick, efficient manner.

"Now, everyone, please enjoy the rest of your evening," he yelled over the crowd. "And be sure to thank any or all members of the Spencer family for their generosity and hospitality."

Dax took a step forward and held his hand out for Violet. Once again she slid her delicate hand in his, and he assisted her down from the stage. The moment she landed at the bottom he released her, but he could honestly admit he didn't want to.

Why was he having such a strong reaction to her? And why was he letting himself?

His eyes darted around and immediately landed on his parents and sister. They were all smiling at him like they knew something he didn't. Only it was the complete opposite—he was the one keeping a big secret.

His dad came forward. "Son, I'm really proud of you."

His father's words, coupled with a firm hand on Dax's shoulder, had a lump forming in his throat. He was pleased with his dad's words, but as his father beamed at Violet, too, that lump of guilt continued to grow. Yet something else grew right alongside it—something for Violet he couldn't quite put a label on and he wasn't even sure he should try. He'd felt something shift tonight—he and Violet seemed to anticipate what the other needed and stepped in to help. When he'd asked Violet to play pretend with him, he'd never imagined a real closeness would form.

"Thanks, Dad." Dax returned his dad's smile and tried to concentrate on his family and not Violet, who politely made an exit and started heading across the room. "I'm really glad you guys could be here for this."

"We wouldn't miss it," his mom said as she came up to his side and wrapped an arm around his waist. She barely reached his shoulder. "I'm going to hate when we have to leave at the end of next week."

"We can always stay longer," Clara suggested.

Dax met her gaze and she shot him a wink. "You know you'll be sad to see us go."

"Of course I will," he agreed. And he would, but he'd also be glad to have this burden lifted and tell the truth once they returned home. "And my spare room will be open for you all anytime you want to come back."

"I hope to come back soon to see you and Violet for an even longer visit." His mom looked up at him with way too much hope in her eyes and he didn't have the heart to say another word. This would all be over soon and he could rid himself of the mounting guilt and the heavy dose of shame.

There certainly wouldn't be anything more between him and Violet Spencer.

"I promise," Violet assured Rachel. "I've got it. You go on home."

Rachel glanced around at the empty barn. Violet had tried for the past thirty minutes to get her to go on home to her new husband and relax. Rachel had done all of the pre-party planning and Violet was too worked up anyway to head home. She needed some quiet time and to work through her thoughts for a bit after that surprise announcement Dax had made.

Between the sweet gesture and that smile he'd turned on her, she'd nearly melted into a puddle onstage, but then she'd quickly reminded herself that nothing they were doing was real.

The fact that he'd decided to raise money for a youth program did something to her she couldn't deny. She had to thank him and she had to make a donation. She also wanted to know how she could help beyond bringing kids into her shelter to volunteer.

"There's probably another hour of work," Rachel insisted. "If I stay—"

"If you stay, then we'll both be tired, and you've done more than enough." Violet waved her hands toward the door. "Go on. I promise I can do this part on my own. It's all trash and laundry at this point."

Rachel stifled a yawn and nodded. "I hate to leave but I also hate to turn away such a generous offer when I'm worn out. Jack and I started working on our own main barn this week and there's more than I thought that needed doing. He's such a city boy—learning as he goes. He's a hard worker, but he's still got a lot to learn about livestock."

"Didn't he spend summers with his grandfather on that farm?" Vi asked.

Rachel nodded. "Yes, but he doesn't remember too much. Between the farm and the feedstore, not to mention his new real estate firm, we're spread a little thin now."

Vi smiled. "All the more reason to get home and relax with a nice cup of tea and honey."

Rachel opened her arms and closed the distance between them as she pulled her into an embrace.

"I owe you one," Rachel told her. They'd sent their mom and dad home, and Luke and Jenn needed to get Paisley to bed. Then Erin had left to finish up a children's church lesson for Sunday. "I really appreciate you staying."

Violet eased back and cupped the side of her sister's cheek. "I wouldn't be anywhere else. Unless it's an emergency at the clinic," she tacked on with a chuckle.

Rachel blew out an exasperated sigh. "Well, then, I'm going home to get that tea going because I just want to cuddle on the sofa with Jack, a cozy blanket and Earl Grey."

The image of such a simple, wholesome night in shouldn't make Violet jealous. She was happy for both of her sisters for finding true love. Rachel had crushed on the boy next door years ago, only to have him come back home to settle his grandfather's estate, and that youthful crush had turned into a full-blown love.

Once her sister was gone, Violet pressed her hands to the small of her back and twisted one way, then the other. She toed off her heeled sandals; she figured she'd get around quicker barefoot on these concrete floors than clunking around in those. She'd had enough of them for one night, especially when she was used to her sneakers and scrubs.

Violet went to the back and wheeled out one of the two-tiered carts. She pushed it alongside the first table and started removing the decor, first the floral pieces and rows of carefully hidden twinkle lights within all the greenery, then the table runners. She moved from one table to the next doing the same, and by the third table she still didn't have a clearer picture in her head of what to think about Dax. Her thoughts and emotions seemed to run from one end of her mind to the other, like they were trying to choose the winning team. Was he a good guy or not?

Clearly he wasn't a *bad* guy. There wasn't a doubt he was one of the good ones. But was he the guy for her? And was she even ready for one after her last disastrous breakup?

"Get it together, Violet," she murmured, plucking the stems from the vase.

"Do you always talk to yourself?"

Vi squealed and spun around, extending the twigs in her hand like a sword for the intruder she hadn't heard come in.

Dax strode toward her like he hadn't just given her a heart attack.

"You're not threatening an officer of the law with foliage, are you?" he asked, gesturing to her weapon of choice.

That signature smirk of his might be cute and enticing to other women, but she was immune to his charms. And she didn't like being terrified out of her mind late at night under any circumstance.

"What in the world are you doing back here?" she asked, dropping the bundle onto the cart.

"Figured you could use help cleaning up." He glanced around and nodded. "Looks like I was right. Where did everyone go?"

"Rach sent Mom and Dad home. Erin and Jenn were busy, and I actually just sent Rachel home because she looked dead on her feet."

Dax had closed in on her now, and only the cart separated them. He crossed his arms and she noted that he'd changed from his uniform to a simple blue T-shirt and jeans. His hair had a slight curl to the ends and she scolded herself for wondering if the texture was coarse or soft.

His hair, or any other aspect of his personal life, was none of her concern. Fake relationship or not, there was no need to be anything other than surface acquaintances.

"Where can I help?" he asked, glancing from the cart to the table, then to her.

Violet shook her head. "I don't expect you to clean up after a party you paid to have. That's not how this works."

"That's how I work," he retorted.

There went that grin again, and her insides did some fluttering dance that she did not appreciate one bit. Her nerves were doing entirely too much quivering where this man was concerned. How did one look from those heavy-lidded eyes or one featherlight touch from his soft fingertips get to her? And those generous gestures he'd made lately… If he had a heart that big, what else was he doing that she knew nothing about?

"I had no idea you'd be here alone," he added. "So if you're uncomfortable, I can go."

Violet felt like a jerk for trying to push him away when his heart truly seemed to be in the right place. She wasn't afraid to be alone with him, other than the fact her emotions were starting to get jumbled and much too confusing.

"If you insist on helping, I'm just taking the decorations off the tables and putting them on the cart. Then I'll take the table runners and tablecloths back to the laundry area. Mom will come over in the morning to wash them. I have to take out the trash and sweep. It sounds like a lot, but it's not bad."

"Even better with an extra set of hands," he replied.

Without hesitation, he turned to one of the round tables and started disassembling. She stared at his back for just a moment, trying to gather her thoughts and find the right words. Sometimes keeping things simple was the best approach.

"Thank you."

He stilled with a bundle of greenery in one hand and a glass vase in the other as he glanced over his shoulder. "For what?"

"Well, this for starters, but for the youth program you want to start."

He straightened and turned, taking his time

to put each item in its proper place on the cart. When he directed his attention back to her, he pinned her with that piercing stare that never failed to mesmerize her. He had the most striking shade of blue eyes she'd ever seen and if she wasn't careful, she'd get lost in them. Or perhaps she already had.

"I should be thanking you for bringing it to my attention," he countered. "I had no idea there was such a need."

"I didn't do anything."

Violet sighed and got back to work. The sooner she was out of this space with him, the better for her nerves. He was too nice, too comforting with those deep, slow words of his, and much too giving. The more she understood and got to know about him, the more she found that he did have a servant's heart.

A heart that was still healing from the loss of his wife, and he'd made it perfectly clear he was only wanting a fresh start and not a replacement for his late wife.

"When I met Oliver, it got my mind working," he told her. "I know there are several foster kids in the area and there are many teens that are often getting into a bit of mischief. Nothing major, but if we don't give them another outlet and start with positive reinforcements at a younger age, there's a high percentage for them to get into more trouble down the road."

Violet concentrated on her task and not that deep voice that was almost soothing. Were her hands shaking? They were just having a conversation for pity's sake. A conversation on a topic that clearly had touched his heart like it had hers.

"I only thought of the idea because I need help with the shelter and can't afford to pay everyone," she explained. "Most kids love animals, so I posted for volunteers at the school. But it's the kids who are sometimes neglected who seem to have a special bond with the animals and tend to stick around. I've only been doing this a couple of months, but I have an online volunteer form and I also keep a paper copy for the kids who don't have computer access."

Violet finished clearing off the table and started to ease the cart to the next table between her and Dax, but stopped short when she spotted him simply staring at her—and he'd moved closer than she'd realized, like he was in some stealth mode.

"What?" she asked, her hands gripping the handles.

"Is there anything you can't do?"

She blinked. "Excuse me?"

"You save animals, you saved me from my

family, you're saving teens from getting into trouble…"

When he trailed off, he pulled in a deep breath and rested his hands on his hips. But that gaze never wavered.

"I'm just surprised," he finally added.

Violet jerked. "You're surprised that I'm nice?"

"That didn't come out right," he corrected. "I didn't realize you had so many layers, but each one that gets revealed is even better than the last."

Her heart clenched. Nobody had ever described her in that way before. Not even her ex after years of dating. How was it that Dax seemed to know her better in less than a week?

"I only try to fix a need when I see it." She maneuvered around the table to the next one and started removing the centerpiece. "I was in desperate need of some help, too, so it's really a win-win for all of us so long as this continues to work out well."

Again, he looked at her as if he could see her every thought and deepest secret. Considering he was her only secret, there wasn't much she was hiding, but she wondered what he was thinking with the way that intense gaze remained locked in place.

"You keep staring at me and I can't tell if that's the face you make when you're dealing with criminals or just when you're deep in thought."

Violet laughed at her own little joke, but not Dax. He didn't even crack a smile.

"You remind me of Junie."

Violet paused and rested her hands on the edge of the metal cart. "Your wife?"

He nodded. "I thought you two were total opposites, but there's something about you that is so her. It just hit me out of nowhere."

"I haven't heard you talk much about her," Violet stated. "Not that we've been together much."

Now he smiled. There was a layer of sadness, but more than anything she saw love.

"June. She had the biggest heart of anyone I knew." His eyes darted away as he spoke, as if the memories were replaying right before him. "She'd try to save anyone or anything. If we had a housefly, she'd find a way to get it outside without killing it. She always wanted those around her to be happy above all else. Her needs never mattered. I'd never met anyone like her."

He directed that penetrating look right back at her. Did that mean he hadn't met anyone like June until Violet? How should she take the unspoken words that seemed to hover between them?

This entire night seemed to have shifted their

dynamics—she wasn't sure how or why—but here they were.

"She sounds lovely." Violet eased around the cart and kept working. "How long were you two married?" Vi quickly glanced at him and added, "You don't have to talk about her if that's too painful."

"Not at all." Dax picked up the side arrangement and took it apart, handing her each piece to organize on the shelves of the cart. "Talking about her is the best way to keep her memory alive. We were married about ten years. She painted every room in our first apartment at least twice until she found the perfect shade. The woman never met a color she didn't like. The brighter the better."

He handed her more pieces and she placed them neatly with the others. They worked as a fluid team, as if they'd torn down decorations many times before.

"She sounds like Erin," Violet told him. "I didn't know whether that was a youngest child thing or because she teaches elementary school."

"My wife worked in an office for a landscaping company, so I have no idea where she got it from." He laughed. "I finally just gave up trying to figure it out. When I'd come home and the yellow walls were suddenly blue, I just went with it."

Violet couldn't help but smile. The love radiating from his voice couldn't be denied or ignored. She couldn't imagine finding something so pure and genuine. At one time she thought she'd done just that, but that entire world had been built on nothing but lies.

Chance had played her and she'd fallen for every single lie he'd told her. In the end, she'd discovered he'd wanted money he thought she'd have because of all the land her family owned. He'd even tried to talk her into joint accounts. That had been her first red flag.

Pushing aside that period of naivety, Violet turned to grab whatever else Dax had ready for her. But she sorely misjudged the distance and gripped hold of his free hand instead. That clutch had her attention and his, too, considering his eyes jerked to hers. The only thing between them was a cart of party decor and a lie that continued to lock them together.

Dax shifted, turning his hand under hers. The roughness of his palm tickled her skin and she sucked in a breath, holding it in as she anticipated his next move or word.

"Maybe that's why I keep getting pulled in with you," he murmured, keeping his focus on their hands. "You seem too familiar. Too comfortable."

Oh, no. He couldn't be catching feelings…

could he? Because if she was confused, and he thought he might be forming an emotional connection they hadn't planned on, then this could lead to a disaster.

"Dax." She tried to sound firm, but her voice came out on a whisper. "We're not anything other than temporary. The way you looked at me earlier tonight and the way you are now... I just don't see how we can keep up this charade if we can't keep it straight ourselves."

He eased his hand from hers and raked his fingers through his wavy hair, making it stand on end. But he nodded in agreement and offered one of his signature grins like nothing had ever happened.

"You're right." He dived right back into disassembling the next table. "We've got just over a week left and we can't do this if we're confusing ourselves. I just got caught up in the moment."

She understood that, but she didn't understand the moment before the party when it seemed like he'd been about to kiss her. She didn't understand the moment they'd just had or the way he had her stomach, her mind and her heart all in knots.

And she wasn't about to bring any of those topics out into the open. She'd agreed to two weeks and that was all she could do. She had plenty on her plate already and she'd gotten out of a deceitful relationship so why on earth did she think it a good idea to try to jump into one that didn't have one shred of truth to it?

No. There was simply too much wedged between them for her and Dax to move beyond this. They would sever this union soon and she'd do all she could to help with the youth program, but that was where their joint ventures would end.

Chapter Eleven

"I'd say the repairs will be done by the end of the week since all the parts came in this morning. Just wanted to keep you in the loop."

Dax listened to Bill, the local auto shop owner. Thankfully the damage to his cruiser wasn't too bad, far less than he'd imagined, and it would be fixed sooner than expected. He hadn't asked about Violet's car but he imagined hers wouldn't be too long either—he hoped.

"I appreciate the update," Dax said.

The owner promised to deliver the vehicle as soon as it was finished and disconnected the call. At least that bit of good news distracted him for a few minutes because all he'd been able to think about since last night was Violet and how far out of control he'd let his emotions go. He'd allowed himself to get wrapped up in Violet's sweetness and memories of his late June.

And Violet hadn't been wrong. Before the party started he'd wanted to kiss her. He was human—he couldn't help how he felt. But should he feel guilty for having these thoughts? For the first time since being a widower, he had an interest in someone. Could he trust those feelings? Or was he simply getting caught up in the pretense he and Violet had put in place?

He glanced at his desk and the empty cup of coffee. He wasn't sure another cup of office sludge would help his nerves. He had no clue what they kept stocked here, but it was terrible. He'd never been a coffee snob before. So long as it was hot, black and had caffeine, that was all he'd cared about. Maybe this bag was old or something. Not that he had time to worry about the office coffee brand.

Dax blew out a sigh, picked up his mug and stood just as his father stepped through the doorway.

"Dad." Dax greeted him with a smile. "What are you doing here?"

"Thought I'd come by and see my son." Mike Adams slid his dark brown cowboy hat off and held the brim with both hands as he crossed the threshold. "If you're not too busy, that is."

"Not at all," Dax assured him. "It's been a slow morning. Are you trying to escape the ladies?"

His father chuckled. "No. They're off to a brunch with Violet."

Brunch with Violet. After the manner in which

things had transpired last night and that whole new level of cozy—and perhaps awkward—way they'd left things, Dax wasn't so sure he was comfortable with Vi and Clara chatting it up this morning. There wasn't much he could do about it now. He just hoped Violet could hold her own. Clara could be overbearing at times.

"Why the scowl?"

His father's words pulled Dax from his thoughts.

"You're not worried about them getting together, are you?" he asked.

Dax nodded. "Honestly, yes. You know how Clara can be."

With a shrug, his father simply sighed. "Yeah, well, if Violet is going to be around this family, she'll just have to get used to your sister and mother. Besides, Violet seems like the type of woman who can take care of herself."

First of all, Violet wasn't going to be in the family long, but those words had to remain unsaid. Second, he assumed she could take care of herself, but how would he know for sure? All he ever saw was her taking care of everyone else. And that was what irked him through this entire ordeal. Never once did he see her doing anything for herself or putting her needs above anyone else's. She cared for animals and youth, her family and now him. Did she have any downtime that she took just for herself? Did she ever schedule anything fun or a day off? He doubted it.

"They'll be just fine," his father assured him, with a pat on his shoulder. He stepped on into the office and glanced around. "Small space. I don't know I'd be able to sit in here all day."

Dax chuckled as he stepped aside and put his mug back on his desk. "Well, I'm not in here all day. I'm typically out in the town meeting new people or dealing with issues."

His dad stopped at the photo on the wall and gestured with his hat. "You look just like him."

"So I've heard."

"From the stories I've been told, you act like him, too." His father turned with a smile. "You come across as tough, and you are when you need to be, but you're soft and genuinely want to help people."

"There's no other job I'd want to do," Dax admitted. "I needed a fresh start, so when this position opened, I really felt like God opened the door for me."

"I believe He did. As hard as it was to see you go, and to see your mother cry, I know this is good for you. June wouldn't have wanted you to stay in a place that kept you in a time of grief. She'd want you happy. I hope I'm not overstepping, but I also think she'd like Violet. Something about her reminds me of June."

A niggling ache settled deep. Was that because his own emotions paralleled what his father had said or because there was actually some truth to the words? If his father noticed it, too, did that mean Violet and June *were* of a similar nature?

They were, he decided, but they were also two different women with two very distinct personalities.

"I was about to grab some coffee. Care to join me?" Dax offered.

Granted he had been planning to head to the break room, but since his dad was here, he'd much rather go to the café on the corner. He could use something with actual flavor and the fresh air wouldn't hurt, either.

His dad nodded. "Sure."

Dax led the way out of the office and waved to the dispatcher as he moved through the open lobby area. The moment he opened the door, warm summer sunshine hit his face, instantly boosting his mood. He'd been conflicted all morning. Part of him just wanted to come clean with his parents and sister. The other part told him to wait until they were home. They were all so happy for him and so at peace with the life he'd found here.

"I see why you like this town," his dad stated as they started down the block.

The cozy, colorful storefronts all welcomed shoppers and visitors. Boutiques, antique shops, restaurants… Rosewood Valley seemed to have it all. American flags waved from light poles along either side of the road. Fat pots overflowing with a variety of flowers and greenery sat about every ten feet. The city council really took pride in making the whole town look beautiful.

"Hi, Sheriff."

Dax waved across the street to an elderly man who'd yelled his greeting. Which in turn got the attention of a few other people who waved and smiled in his direction.

"You seem to be well-liked," his dad commented as they neared the café. "Obviously they know a good man when they see one."

"So far I haven't run into any issues. Most people are friendly and the others I just don't hear from."

"Well, from what I've seen of the Spencer family, they're good people."

Dax wholeheartedly agreed. Well before he'd met Violet face-to-face, or bumper-to-grill, he'd met a couple members of the family and had nothing but good experiences with them. Their stellar reputation preceded them.

"I have to say, your mother is so relieved to know you've found happiness again," his dad went on. "She was worried on our way out here about just how we'd find you. She thought for sure your video calls were all a front and you were in some bare apartment living off junk food and crying into your pillow at night."

Dax laughed. "Are you serious?"

"Well, she didn't use those exact words, but you know how Mom worries and she didn't know if you had friends yet."

Dax stopped in front of the café and adjusted his own hat against the sun's rays. "I told you all for the few months I've been here that I was fine. I promise, I'm good. I have enough to keep busy and I love this town. There's always something going on and plenty of people to socialize with. I certainly am not crying into my pillow at night. There have been a few times my dinners have been junk, but don't tell Mom."

His dad gave a curt nod and reached for the café door handle. "Not a word. And for that matter, I had a cupcake before I came to meet you once she was out the door. The guesthouse we're staying in brought fresh pastries and I couldn't turn those down."

Dax chuckled as he stepped through the open door and led his dad inside. The quaint spot was a popular hangout for people of all ages, from teens with after-school homework to retirees getting together to talk politics thinking they could solve the world's problems over a vanilla latte.

"Oops. We've been spotted."

Dax's father pointed toward the back where his mother was waving and smiling.

Great. He didn't know the ladies had come here for their brunch. He just assumed they'd gone to one of the other restaurants in town. Well, Dax couldn't exactly turn and run now or he'd look guilty of something—which he was. Now he looked like he'd followed them and was snooping.

"We can just get ours to go," Dax told his dad. "Let's leave them to their talk."

"Oh, I don't want in the middle of that, either."

At least they were on the same page.

But Clara turned, then Violet turned, and suddenly three sets of eyes were on them. Now Clara and his mother were both waving them over and Violet seemed to force a grin before picking up her cup of orange juice and taking a sip.

Dax willed his radio to go off or his cell. Anything to get him out of this restaurant—but that would leave Violet stuck with his whole family. Was she also looking for a way out? Had she agreed to this only to appease them or to further their plan? She was such a people pleaser that he didn't imagine she'd say no if she didn't have to.

"We better at least say hi and then we can

excuse ourselves and let them get back to their girls' day," his father muttered.

Dax followed his dad as they made their way through the crowd. There were mirrors along the back wall and a bench that stretched the entire length with various tables in front. The ladies were seated at the far left and thankfully there were no seats available.

To Dax's surprise, as he got closer, it wasn't worry or a need to escape that he saw in Violet's eyes. No, she seemed to be truly enjoying herself. Her eyes sparkled and she even leaned over and whispered something to his sister that made Clara laugh.

Oh, no. Did those two already have an inside joke? Were they bonding? This didn't bode well for the impending "breakup" they had at the end of next week. He hadn't even taken into consideration how Violet would get along with his family, but he wasn't surprised. There wasn't any doubt that Clara and Violet had swapped stories considering they were both in the medical field. Granted Clara helped deliver babies, but Dax was sure there was some healthcare bonding going on.

"Ladies," his father greeted as they stood before the table. "You all look lovely today."

"Did you guys follow us?" Clara smirked.

"Not hardly." Dax snorted. "Dad stopped by the station and we decided to grab a cup of coffee."

"Don't worry, we're not staying," his dad tacked on.

"You're more than welcome." His mom glanced around for another chair. "I can try to find another chair to pull over."

"No." Dax wasn't about to join this party. "I'm on duty and can't stick around."

"Violet invited us all to dinner tomorrow," his mom announced.

With all the hustle and bustle of the café, Dax thought for sure he'd heard her wrong. There was no way Violet would take this farce one step further by planning a family dinner in her home. She was busy with her own event coming up next week, and she wouldn't do something like this without discussing with him first.

When his eyes met hers, she merely smiled and lifted a shoulder.

"We're using your kitchen," Violet informed him. "It's bigger than mine."

But of course they were. Why wouldn't they?

She had made plans without checking with him first. Weren't they keeping things simple and just trying to fly through these days as a couple? Or maybe they'd already crossed a line and now he and Violet would have to figure the best way to deal with how fast their families were embracing this relationship.

A whole family gathering at his new house where he wanted to make new memories…

Well, at least this would all be temporary and these memories wouldn't soak into the walls and every crevice of the place where he wanted to start his new chapter. These memories wouldn't hurt to look back on and more than likely, he'd get a chuckle out of them one day…he hoped.

As much as he wanted to be annoyed with Violet not asking him first, he only had himself to blame because she was only doing what he'd asked of her…giving his family peace of mind that Dax was doing just fine here.

Dax's radio came to life with his dispatcher requesting a unit to the old warehouse by the river where some teens were spotted sneaking in. Dax turned from the table and reached up to tap the piece clipped to his shoulder, informing them he was two minutes away and would report.

"Sorry, guys." He focused back on his family and Violet. "I'll have to catch up at dinner tomorrow."

"You go," his father told him. "I'll get my coffee, wander about town and see what I can get into."

Dax gave his father a pat on his back before leaning down to kiss his mother on the cheek. He moved to do the same to his sister, then quickly realized his mistake. But he was in it now and he couldn't stop or ignore Violet or this whole relationship would look suspicious.

He came around to her side of the table and her eyes widened as they met his. The moment he bent down, he didn't even try to stop himself. Dax leaned right in and feathered his lips across her soft skin. He'd known even before touching her that she'd be soft, but now was not the time or the place to analyze the innocent gesture.

Nor could he think about that swift intake of her breath or the way she continued to stare at him like something had shifted inside her as well.

Without another word, he moved through the café and out the door into the warm sunshine. He needed to focus on his job and not the way guilt gnawed at his gut.

Guilt from the lies to his family and guilt for his late wife because Dax could no longer deny his attraction to Violet, and he had no clue how to proceed with this. Which was why he should focus solely on his professional life—because his personal life was spinning out of control.

Chapter Twelve

"Did you hear me? Violet?"

Violet blinked and tried to focus on Clara, but her mind was still on that peck on her cheek from earlier today. Since Dax had left the café, she'd been in a daze. She'd gone into the clinic, seen her patients and was now at the shelter where Clara insisted on coming to help prepare for Pets in the Park next week.

"I'm sorry." Violet turned her attention back to the desk where the layout of the park had a mock-up of the event drawn out. "My mind is in a million different directions. I always feel like I'm in crunch mode the week before this fundraiser."

"No worries." Clara patted her arm. "It's because you care. I was just saying—do you always have the face-painting station near the cotton candy truck?"

"The cotton candy truck is new this year."

Clara pursed her lips and stared down at the drawing.

"What are you thinking?" Violet asked. "I'm open to suggestions."

"I was just thinking the lines might get backed up for both and then the crowd would be more in that area and not circulating."

Violet scanned the drawing and nodded in agreement. "I hadn't thought of that. This is why I need fresh eyes on these things. There are so many elements to make this run smooth and I'm always trying to add just a few new things each year to keep it fresh and fun, but still have the main focus on the animals and the adoptions."

"This all looks amazing," Clara stated. "I'm glad we'll still be in town for it."

Honestly, Violet was, too. During just the little time she'd spent with Dax's family, she'd really enjoyed herself, from the farm-to-table event, where their families seemed to just mesh well, to their brunch earlier today. Violet would be sad to see them go.

If there was a real relationship happening, she could see potential with Dax, but that was not the case. There was nothing legitimate here and this path she was walking was starting to turn into a very fine line. She should have stuck to her original plan and purposely stayed busy, or at least said she didn't have any free time. That way she wouldn't have had all this time with his family or even alone time with him. She wouldn't have made these chinks in her armor she'd kept so perfectly in place since she'd broken things off with Chance.

Clara eyed her again. "I hear my brother wants a dog."

Violet straightened from the desk and smiled.

"He does," Violet confirmed. "He came by and looked at a few, but he's decided on Colt. I thought he would have picked him up before now but I know he's been busy... Or he might have gotten scared away."

Clara leaned a hip on the desk and tucked her blond hair behind her ears. "I don't think anything scares Dax. Well, other than getting his heart broken again. But a dog? No way. He said once he got settled here he would be getting a pet so I know he's ready. It's the girlfriend none of us expected."

Yeah. Violet hadn't expected that whole girlfriend part, either. "Tell me about his wife."

Where did that come from?

Violet hadn't meant to say it. Of course she'd wondered about Dax's past—that was just human nature. Since he'd told her she reminded him of his late wife, Violet couldn't help but wonder how they were similar. She hadn't meant to dig deeper with Clara, though.

"Funny you should ask." Clara smirked a little. "Mom and Dad keep saying how you remind them of June. I see what they're talking about, but I also see how different you two are. It's clear my brother's type is a giving woman with a big heart and someone who is selfless. But then you're more bold and assertive. June wasn't meek, but she was quiet and reserved and... I don't think this is coming out right."

Clara winced and Violet couldn't help but laugh as she set a hand on her arm for reassurance. "You're fine and I'm not offended. I grew up with three sisters. We're all assertive because we were all trying to make our voices heard."

"I can't even imagine having three sisters." Clara eased farther onto the desk and sighed. "Having an overprotective twin brother was rough at times, but I always thought a sister would be so cool. I couldn't exactly go to Dax with boyfriend issues in school because he'd intervene or say something to the guy. I couldn't get sisterly advice on a dress for prom or how to cut my hair. I was so happy when June came along and I had someone to talk to. I mean, I always had my mother, but sometimes you just want someone your age, you know?"

Violet nodded. "I get it. I'm sure the loss of June was devastating for the entire family."

Clara's brow creased. "It was, but we were so concerned about Dax that our own feelings had to take a back seat."

Violet couldn't imagine Dax broken and in a dark place, but Vi knew how Jenn had been when she'd lost her husband. Jenn had fled Rosewood Valley for three years, trying to run from the pain. Violet didn't think Dax was running by coming here, though. She truly believed he needed a fresh start to move on and heal, and there was nothing wrong with that. Everyone had to grieve at their own pace and in their own way.

"You're good for him," Clara went on. "This town, the job, but especially you. All these pieces God laid in place for Dax are just perfect. Of course, I still worry because I'm the older sister by a few minutes." She grinned. "I can't help myself. I just love him so much and want him to find happiness again, and despite getting on my nerves at times, he really is one of the best guys."

That lump in Vi's throat seemed to grow. The lump that wouldn't allow the truth to slip out. The lump that prevented her from saying anything because she didn't know what to say at this point. Each day that passed was another day that she fell in deeper with this family and maybe even a bit more with Dax, if she was being honest with herself. She didn't want to find him intriguing or attractive or anything else positive. She wanted to keep her heart guarded.

"He actually started a scholarship at the local high school where he and June graduated," Clara went on, oblivious to Violet's thoughts. "June came from a family that didn't have a lot and she couldn't go to college, which she always regretted. Dax wanted to do something to keep her name alive and that's the only way he knew how."

Great. Another endearing quality that only made him more commendable. She didn't need more reasons to like him. She needed to find a way out of this without hurt feelings or broken hearts.

"How did June pass?" Violet asked. "If you don't mind my asking."

Clara's eyes welled up and she chewed on her bottom lip for a moment, almost as if to compose herself, but then she gave a slight nod and blew out a sigh. "A distracted driver. So senseless and tragic. Dax had just gotten to work and June was on her way home from work. Some lady on her phone went left of center and hit June. She died on impact and the other driver was taken to the hospital with a few injuries, but nothing life-threatening."

Violet's gut clenched. How awful... None of this seemed fair, but Violet knew life was never promised to be fair. Life was up-and-down and messy. But there were beautiful moments woven in between the heartache, and that's what people had to cling to.

Then she remembered how angry Dax had been when she'd rear-ended him and he'd muttered something about being on her phone and not paying attention. Her heart sank and she wished she could recall what she had said, if anything. She hoped she hadn't said something sarcastic or made light of the situation, especially now knowing his backstory. Violet felt so foolish and wanted to comfort Dax. Even though time had passed since that day, she found herself wanting to assure him she was here if he needed a friend.

Oh, no. It was happening. And by *it* she meant she'd caught some of those feelings she'd promised herself she wouldn't catch. Just a week ago she couldn't stand the man and now she wanted to hug him and make sure he knew everything would be okay.

"So." Clara smacked her palms on the tops of her thighs. "Show me the dog my brother was considering. I'm a great judge of character."

Yes. A much better subject than heartache and grieving. Violet could get on board with shifting topic to her rescues. Besides, she figured she'd pried enough into Dax's personal life. She could have just asked him how June had passed and he likely would have told her, but she hadn't intended to dive any deeper until now.

"Colt's right outside," Violet stated, gesturing toward the exit.

The moment Violet opened the office door, the chaotic surround sound of barking hit them. Vi didn't think anything of it, but Clara laughed.

"Is it always like this?" she yelled over the noise.

"Pretty much." Violet led the way toward the back hallway that would take them to the play yard. "They sleep at night and some nap during the day, but when people are here, they want all the attention."

"I'd be tempted to take them all home," Clara told her as she followed.

"It's difficult," Violet admitted. "Do you have any pets?"

"I don't. Since I live alone and I'm a full-time nurse, plus there are weekends I'm on call, I don't think it's fair to leave an animal alone that long. I mean, I'd get a cat, but then Dax could never visit me."

Violet nodded, unlocked the back door and held it open for Clara to pass.

"The dogs might jump," she warned.

"Oh, I'll be fine," Clara assured her. "Let's see what you've got. I'm sure I can pick out which one he's considering."

Violet hung back while the mass of dogs greeted the newcomer with hops of excitement and slobbery kisses. Vi started to apologize, because she always felt like these were her children, but with a smile on her face and loving pats to each animal, Clara seemed to be doing just fine.

"You're quite an animal lover yourself," Violet pointed out.

"I am," she admitted. "We always had at least one dog, if not two, growing up. When I find the right man and settle down, he better buckle up because we are having a houseful of pets."

Violet loved that attitude and wished more people would consider taking in these precious pets. Too many were left abandoned or treated as temporary fun. Having an animal was at least a decade-long commitment but often more.

"I'm going to guess that he liked this one."

Violet followed Clara's pointer finger and nodded. She'd found Colt. "I'm impressed. He played ball with Colt for a while the other day."

"Then he'll definitely be back to get him."

Clara seemed confident and Violet hoped that was the case. She truly felt Dax and Colt were a perfect match. She didn't doubt Dax would get the supplies and contact her when he was ready. But she wouldn't push the union.

Like a human relationship, the fit couldn't

be forced. The connection was either there or it wasn't.

"Can I ask you something?" Clara continued to divide her attention between Colt and a couple of the other older dogs.

"Of course," Violet replied, though a question like that seemed loaded, especially considering the delicate circumstances.

"Do you know Ben?"

Ben?

Violet blinked. Clara wasn't going to ask about her and Dax? She was relieved, but shocked.

"Ben at the station?" Violet asked, holding her hand to shield the sun from her eyes.

Clara nodded. "It's silly, but when I stopped by the other day I met him."

Oh, really? Wasn't this interesting…

Violet couldn't help but wonder if Dax knew about Clara asking after his deputy or if this was a girl secret. Regardless, Violet thought it was rather sweet.

"Ben is a great guy," Violet told her. "He went to school with my sister Erin so he's a little younger than me. He has a pretty big family and owns a very small ranch. Deals more with horses than cattle. He helps with his parents quite a bit, too. Do I need to put in a good word for you? I think he's single."

Clara shrugged and stood straight up. "I'm

not sure," she sighed, propping her hands on her hips. "I don't plan on staying here and I'm only asking because he's cute so that seems really shallow of me."

Violet understood that instant physical attraction. Wasn't that what drew most people in initially?

"There's no shame in feeling that way," she assured Clara. "I thought Dax was handsome the first time I saw him."

Not a lie, but probably not something she wanted getting back to him, either. The last thing he needed was to think she wanted more than she was saying.

"I shouldn't have said anything." Clara waved a hand. "Forget I mentioned it. I mean, I'm leaving at the end of next week and I'm not sure when I'll be back."

"Doesn't mean you can't have a long-distance friendship," Violet suggested.

Clara pursed her lips and didn't turn down the idea, so Vi figured maybe she could see what she could do for this situation.

Then she realized she'd be meddling, and wasn't that the one thing she didn't want people doing for her? That was exactly how she got herself into this ordeal to begin with. How she found herself getting deeper and deeper with not only Dax, but also his family, which she'd never taken into consideration. She'd given the whole fake-dating scenario about three minutes of her thoughts before agreeing, though, so she hadn't had much time to roll the idea around in her head.

Why did life have to be so complicated and confusing? Violet didn't know how people got through difficult times without faith and God. She really didn't know what else she could rely on for strength. She did know, however, that she needed to pray over this entire situation because in the end—and there would be an end—she sincerely hoped nobody ended up with a broken heart.

Chapter Thirteen

"You didn't have to do this."

Dax flattened his palms on the center island of his kitchen while Violet chopped fresh herbs for the potatoes. He'd offered to help multiple times and she'd declined each time. So he remained in the room for moral support, but he wasn't going to leave her to make dinner for his family all by herself.

"I'm aware I don't," she stated, focusing on her task without looking up. "Your mom and sister were talking about the farm-to-table events and I was telling them how growing up we grew most everything we ate and cooked from that. I told them about various dishes and how we would also do canning and sell goods at the farmers market. One thing led to another and I offered dinner. It's like our farm-to-table, just on a much smaller scale."

"How's the rest of the planning for the fundraiser coming?" he asked. "What else can I do to help?"

A smile spread across her face as she finally glanced up at him. *There. Get her on a topic she absolutely loves and she positively beams.* That kind, giving soul of hers couldn't be contained or put on as a show. Violet was the real deal when it came to those animals. He hadn't been around for her other events, but there wasn't a doubt in his mind this one would be successful because she wouldn't allow it to go off any other way.

"Your sister came by yesterday and gave me a couple ideas," she told him. "She also played with Colt and picked him out immediately as the one you would've connected with."

Dax smiled. "Is that right? I didn't get to the feedstore to pick up all the supplies. I got busy with work and then I thought I should wait for the weekend so I have a couple of days off with him. I'm sorry about that."

"Nothing to be sorry about," she replied. "He will be happy whatever day you bring him home."

Violet placed her knife on the counter and scooped the chopped rosemary into a pile and sprinkled it over the cubed potatoes on the cooking sheet. He kept his eyes on her delicate hands, wondering why he was so enamored of something so simple as watching her cook.

He and Junie hadn't spent much time in the kitchen together. He'd always been on second or third shift for work and she worked during the daytime. So this right here—he couldn't pinpoint what he was feeling, but the stirrings he'd been having for several days now continued to churn.

What if this didn't have to be temporary? What if they tried to actually date and nobody had to know this was all a sham? Then if they decided to "break up" for real, they would be the only ones who knew.

"Dax?"

He shook away the thoughts and shifted his attention back to her. "I'm sorry. What?"

"You have a weird look on your face." She scrunched her nose slightly as her brows drew in. "You okay?"

Not really, but what could he say? That she was the first woman he had feelings for since his wife passed? That he actually wanted to date her and see if this whole thing could be something more? That she intrigued him more than she frustrated him? He really wasn't sure what to say because all of this was so far outside of his wheelhouse, he had no reference point to look back on. He'd never been a widower with an undeniable attraction before, much less found himself with a desire to start dating again. Was he actually considering this?

He didn't know if the nerves curling in his

stomach were a sign of anticipation or a red flag to abort these crazy thoughts.

"Just thinking," he stated honestly. "What were you saying?"

"I just wanted you to know that I can give Rachel a list of everything you'd need and she can bring it here on her way home from the feedstore whenever you're ready. I can bring Colt to you or you can come to the shelter and pick him up. Whichever you're comfortable with."

"Maybe we can do that tomorrow. Is that okay?"

He didn't think she could get more beautiful, but she did. That radiant smile of hers lit up her entire face. "I'd go right now if you wanted, but we have company coming."

We have company coming. The way those words came out made it sound as if they were a couple hosting a dinner party. But they weren't a couple and none of this was reality. And it couldn't be a reality until he was absolutely sure he was ready to date again. He couldn't risk hurting Violet by admitting his budding feelings without being certain he was ready to act on them.

"Let me get everything in the oven and I'll text Rachel," she said. "I'm so excited for you and Colt."

Of course she was. Her love for these connections was clear and he wondered just how many she'd made over the years. There was so much he wanted to know about her, and to his surprise, he wasn't one bit afraid at his yearning to dive deeper in his study of her.

"When was the last time you dated?" he asked.

Her eyes darted to his as she stilled with the pan of raw chicken in hand. Yeah, that shocked look on her face mimicked his own internal emotions. He had no idea where that question came from, nor did he have a second to think before he spoke.

"I mean, I know you said some guy..." Dax went on. "But wasn't that a while ago?"

Violet nodded. "He was my last serious relationship, and to be honest, that one about did me in. The deceit and lies... I had no idea what was going on and I'd gotten in way too deep. I thought we'd get married and raise a family here. Once I found out the truth, every single one of those dreams just vanished."

The lies. Like the one Dax had purposely pulled her into. But he hadn't asked her to get her heart involved here and he hadn't promised a lifetime together.

"What were the lies?" he couldn't help but ask. Call it an occupational hazard, but he wanted more information and found himself pushing just a bit more.

Violet pursed her lips as she hesitated. Then she turned toward the oven and opened the door. Silence filled the kitchen and he waited. She slid the pan of chicken in, then the potatoes with rosemary, and some sort of veggie casserole. He didn't know if she'd answer or not, but he was going to give her space and time and respect however she responded.

She closed the oven door and reached over the stovetop to set the timer. She stared at the panel for a moment, trying to figure out how it worked. He'd help, but he had no clue himself since he hadn't used it since moving in. After a few pushes and some beeps, she nodded in satisfaction, then turned to face him once again.

"Chance was my real estate agent, so that's how we met. He was quite successful and traveled a lot for work at the time. He conveniently had a girlfriend in another county." Violet crossed her arms and tipped her chin. Defense mode engaged. "I had no idea about her, nor did she know about me. Apparently he was trying to figure out who he wanted to be with. The relationships went on longer than he intended and he just settled right in. He broke my trust, not just of men, but of humanity for a while until I realized God put Chance in my path for a reason and I had to figure out what that reason was."

Dax leaned forward, more than irritated she'd

had to go through such betrayal and hurt, not to mention humiliation, most likely. Dax wouldn't mind having a chat with this Chance character, but that likely wouldn't do anyone any good and none of this really was his business.

"I learned that God has a special plan for me," she told him. "I don't know what it is and I don't know the timing. But I also know I can't force a marriage and a family as much as I want what my parents have. My time will come if that's what's meant to be. And if not, then I have a calling to my work and my service to the community. I can't be upset with that."

Dax listened and just when he thought she couldn't get more remarkable, she proved him wrong. More and more he found himself fascinated and surprised by this invisible pull that kept tugging at him. Could he trust all of this uncharted territory that surrounded him? There was only one way to find out and for the first time in his entire life, he was terrified to step out and try.

Dax opted for more of the truth. He had to inch closer and closer back to his core values and what he believed in. He'd always been a man of integrity and honor, and the fact her ex had led her down a path of deceit made Dax no better at this point. He had to start steering this back around and being the man his parents had raised and the man he could be proud of.

"You're not what I expected."

There. That was one hundred percent honesty. She'd blown him away from their first meeting and continued to do so each time they were together. She wasn't some flighty woman who'd been self-absorbed and in her own world when she'd plowed into him at that intersection. He'd let that moment be colored by the most tragic time in his life, and he'd immediately assumed the worst. Yet she was nothing like he'd thought and everything he hadn't expected.

Violet tipped her head and her high ponytail brushed against her shoulder. With this island between them, he counted that as a blessing. He wondered, if they were a little closer, would he just give in and reach out to see if those blond strands were as soft as he remembered. Again, what right did he have? They'd not even discussed being friends, but he had to believe this was just an unspoken assumption at this point.

When she said nothing, he figured he might as well keep going. The food was cooking and his family hadn't arrived yet. No time like the present.

"I have to be one hundred percent honest with you even if I can't be honest with everyone else right now," he said. "You're more than I thought you'd be when we started all of this. I thought I'd have to avoid you or at least write you one more ticket because you'd purposely do something to spite me."

Her short burst of laughter lightened the mood, which was the very intent he had. He didn't want this to get too heavy but he also had to at least dip his toe and test the waters.

"I appreciate your honesty." Violet let out a sigh and glanced down at the island, then started fidgeting with the plastic tie from the bag of rosemary. "I also appreciate you not writing me another ticket seeing as how I'm still waiting to get my car back and I doubt the car I've borrowed will be able to haul everything for my event. I don't need added stress."

When her green eyes darted back up to his, his breath caught in his throat. If he could fall for someone solely based on beauty, he would've already been gone. But he wasn't shallow and there was so much more to Violet than her authentic appearance.

And he wasn't falling. He was fascinated and intrigued and for the first time since Junie passed, he was ready to try, and that in itself was the biggest step he'd taken.

Chapter Fourteen

"I can't believe you're telling this story."

Violet pressed a hand to her belly as her laughter consumed her. "Oh, leave your sister alone," Vi said, still laughing. "Keep going, Clara."

Dax looked like he wanted to be anywhere but on this front porch with his sister and his parents. Personally, Violet was enjoying the baby Dax stories, but she could see why he wanted a change of topic. The tales rolled from one embarrassing toddler scenario to another and Violet was only glad her sisters weren't here to add their own spin on her childhood memories.

"The neighbor told Mom she would only babysit me, but not Dax," Clara continued. "Unless Mom could promise he would stop streaking out the front door and down the street."

Dax groaned and rubbed his forehead as he leaned against the porch post. Violet couldn't help but feel a little sorry for him, but only because she'd hate her sisters roasting her like this.

Clara pushed the porch swing with the tip of her bare toe and kept the slight momentum going.

After their day in the kitchen, Dax's parents had insisted on cleaning up. Once they were done, they'd joined Dax, Violet and Clara on the porch. Clara and Vi had claimed the porch swing and Dax sat on the top step. His parents had just taken seats in the two rockers his mother had bought earlier. The evening summer breeze lifted the petals on the potted plants his father had bought at the feedstore. Violet's attention landed on the way Mike and Kay held hands between their chairs as they rocked in unison.

This house already had so much love and life in it. She wasn't even the one living here and she had memories. She couldn't imagine how Dax was feeling—well, other than from the embarrassing stories.

"In my defense," Dax grumbled, "that woman kept her house hotter than the surface of the sun. I had to shed some clothes."

"All of them and then run down the street?" Clara laughed.

"I was four, okay?"

"He was a rotten one, that's for sure," his father added. "Many nights his mother would worry what he'd be like as an adult."

"And look at him now." Kay Adams beamed with pride. "We had no reason to worry at all."

"I wasn't worried," his father corrected. "You were. I knew he was just a mischievous boy."

"I don't think that's what you said when he stole a candy bar from the gas station," Clara muttered.

"Oh my word." Dax sat up straighter and turned toward his sister. "I did not steal it. I had it in my hand and forgot to put it on the counter."

"Like I said. Stolen." Clara grinned. Dax scowled.

His twin leaned across the swing toward Violet. "Isn't he cute when he's cranky?"

Violet's eyes met Dax's and he gave that smirk that used to irritate her and now, well, she did find him cute, and she scolded herself for being susceptible. Her attraction went beyond physical looks. He had a caring side and a wounded side that he didn't want people to see or worry about. How could she not find that endearing?

"He is cute," Violet replied, still holding his gaze.

Why lie or pretend? She wasn't faking that part and she really had nothing to lose with her honesty right now.

Dax's smirk turned to a full-fledged grin that spread across his face.

Yeah. She was in some serious trouble. Why did she have to be so drawn to him? The first guy who'd intrigued her so much since Chance, and he seemed to have a heart as guarded as hers was...

"I hear you're getting a dog," his mom stated, pulling Violet's thoughts from the moment. She took in a deep breath and shifted her mind to the present and not some fantasy where she and Dax might enter into a real relationship. Nothing could be built on the foundation of lies and neither of them could trust this—could they? They'd both experienced heartache and been clear that they wanted nothing in the form of a significant other right now.

So here they were. Pretending to be together, yet not together at all, while she wished they were together. But she had to be smart about this. They hadn't known each other long. She'd trusted Chance, fallen for him way too soon, and look where that had got her.

"Violet has several shelter animals and I found one that I'm going to bring home," he replied. "His name is Colt and he's a mix, but mostly wolfhound and mountain dog."

"Oh, I bet he's a big boy." His mom chuckled. "Well, you definitely have the yard for him."

"I'm going to get him tomorrow," Dax told her. "I hope he settles in okay."

"He'll be just fine," Violet assured him.

"Plus your neighbor and girlfriend can help him get settled in," Clara chimed in.

Girlfriend. That term didn't sit well with Violet, but at the same time, she didn't cringe like she had at the beginning.

"Do you need us to help with Pets in the Park on event day?" Clara asked. "I saw one of those cute flyers today in town and I meant to text you and then I got sidetracked. But we plan on being there so feel free to put us to work."

Violet started to answer, but Clara's cell vibrated on the swing between them. Vi didn't mean to be nosy, but when she glanced down and saw Ben's name, she looked back up to see a wide smile on Clara's face. When Clara met Violet's gaze, Clara gave a slight shake of her head, a silent plea to not say anything.

Another secret.

But this one seemed harmless, and it wasn't Violet's business or her place to say a word. She crossed her legs and rested her arm on the side of the swing and glanced around. She stopped short when she caught sight of Dax shooting her a questioning look. He knew something was up.

Violet tried to think of something quick to say to break up the moment that Mike and Kay seemed oblivious to, but Dax's cell chimed and thankfully pulled his attention away.

He fished the device from his pocket and answered.

"Sheriff Adams."

Everyone remained quiet as he listened, but he was on his feet in seconds and moving into the house. Clearly he had to go and something serious was going on. She wondered what it could be. Not too many urgent things happened in Rosewood Valley, which had Violet sending up a silent prayer that all parties involved were okay and that anyone responding to the scene would be okay as well.

Minutes later Dax came right back out the door still in his jeans and T-shirt, but he had his holster and gun strapped on, his radio, his hat and his boots.

"Sorry, guys. We have a situation. Stay as long as you want. I'm not sure when I'll be back."

He seemed to say everything in one quick sentence as he bounded off the porch and down to the driveway. Then he slid behind the wheel of the unmarked car and was gone.

"Well, that must be some situation," his mother gasped. "I don't recall a time when he didn't kiss us goodbye before leaving."

Concern filled Violet, but she couldn't let the worry override her faith. And since Dax had said they could wait as long as they wanted, she intended to do just that.

"I didn't even do anything!"

Wyatt had a grumbling teen with his hands

behind his back as Dax tried to hold back the other. The other teen being Oliver, whom he'd met at Violet's shelter just the other day.

"We weren't doing anything," Oliver insisted.

Dax held on to Oliver's wrists and glanced at Wyatt. When Dax had gotten the call, there had been a whole group of teen boys hanging out at the abandoned warehouse down by the river. By the time Dax showed up, only Oliver and his buddy were left and Dax assumed because these boys were the youngest and not quite teens, they were thrown under the proverbial bus to take the fall.

"You are trespassing," Wyatt informed them. "There are signs posted all over and there's a locked gate, which means you all climbed over the fence. There's also security cameras so you might as well tell us who all you were with or we'll just go look for ourselves."

There were no security cameras, but these kids didn't know that. The warehouse had been a hot spot for illegal activity for a while now and a slight issue Dax had inherited when he'd taken on the job. The fact that Oliver was here only concerned Dax even more. He knew this would devastate Violet, but he hoped she wouldn't have to find out.

"We're just hanging out," the one boy said. "There's nothing to do in this dumb town."

Which was the main reason Dax wanted to get this youth program up and running as soon as possible. Kids were finding things to do that were getting them into trouble and if he and other people in the town, like Violet with her giving heart, could take that energy and use it for good, maybe these kids would get on the right path.

"There *are* things to do," Dax corrected. "And there will be more coming soon. Do you want to learn more about those things or do you want to let older kids continue to get you into trouble?"

Oliver muttered something and Dax leaned down. "What was that?" he asked.

"You're going to tell her, aren't you?" the adolescent said.

Dax's heart clenched for this young boy. He did care what people thought and clearly he respected Violet, which was a big step in the right direction. Dax had to keep him moving in that direction and hope the other boys followed.

"I can leave that up to you," Dax replied, then turned his attention back to the boy Wyatt had. "You want to tell us who else was here?"

Silence filled the old dank area as both boys opted to stare down at their dirty worn sneakers instead of speaking. Dax hadn't figured this would be easy, but he'd hoped.

"That's fine." Dax sighed and started toward

the large opening where the sun cast an orange glow from the beautiful sunset God painted for them this evening. "We'll go out to the patrol cars and call your guardians and let you explain everything, and then they can come down here and pick you guys up."

"Man, why you always gotta call them?" the one boy complained.

"If you didn't do things that were illegal, we wouldn't have to call," Wyatt explained. "Is this the last time you'll be breaking in here?"

"There's no breaking in when there isn't even a door on this side," the youth fired back.

Dax reached his car and turned Oliver around to rest against the back passenger door. Wyatt had his boy at the front of the car so they weren't too close.

"Here's how this is going to go." Dax decided right at this minute to offer this, though he wasn't really giving them a choice. "We will call your guardians and let them know you were caught yet again at the warehouse. But we will also tell them that you're going to be volunteering your time with a business of your choosing in town."

"Are you serious?" The young man with Wyatt groaned and shook his head. "I'm not working for free."

"You can choose where you volunteer," Dax went on, raising his voice just a bit louder. "That way you are helping the owner, plus learning something you could maybe take into the future when you're an adult."

"That's all?" Oliver asked. "That's our punishment?"

"It's a second chance," Dax corrected. "And it's part of a new program we're starting. So are you guys in or do you want to keep getting into trouble and end up somewhere worse than with a kind local business owner who wants to help you be a better version of yourself?"

"I don't wanna work for free. This is stupid," the one boy muttered.

"It doesn't feel like work," Oliver said over his shoulder.

The boy at the front of the car jerked around. "How do you know?"

Oliver shrugged and turned away. "I've been doing some stuff at the animal shelter. I like it."

Wyatt shot Dax a glance and raised his brows. Maybe Wyatt thought Dax had lost his mind, and perhaps this wouldn't work, but he had to try something. He didn't want to just wait and watch and expect these kids to go down the wrong path when he could change the trajectory. This would give youth who found themselves in trouble a chance to do community service—but with the added perk of choosing where they wanted to volunteer.

"There could be worse things than playing with puppies," Dax chimed in.

"You might even like hanging at the auto body shop," Wyatt told him. "I bet you know a thing or two about cars."

That got the boy's attention as he glanced up and gave a slight nod. "I might," he mumbled.

Dax glanced at Wyatt, glad his deputy had known how to reach this kid.

"So we good with this?" Dax asked. "I'll explain when we call your guardians that you guys are going to be doing me a favor by helping to start a new youth program with the sheriff's department. I don't have to go into details tonight."

Wyatt jerked his head around again and Dax knew he was walking a fine line here.

"Why would you do that?" Oliver asked.

"Because everyone needs a second chance and for someone to believe in them. And I'm going to believe you two will do the right thing from here on out." Dax looked from one boy to the next. "Am I right?"

They both nodded and Dax could only hope and pray this would all work out and that he'd made the right decision. Only time would tell.

By the time he got home, Dax felt a bit better about the plan he'd made on the spot. After the phone calls and returning the boys safely to their homes, he and Wyatt had spoken and while Wyatt admitted he'd thought Dax was crazy at first, he ultimately thought the way Dax handled the situation was brilliant.

Having that support from one of his fellow officers was the validation Dax needed. Even though he was the one in charge, there were times he doubted himself. He just had to pretend like he was confident in his decisions because being in an upper level of authority didn't leave room for him to appear vulnerable.

The headlights cut through the dark night as he pulled into his driveway and he did a double take at the sight of Violet's car still there. He'd told everyone to stay as long as they wanted, but he didn't expect to see her there. His family appeared to have left.

When he pulled in beside her, he found himself smiling. Why had she stayed so long? He'd been away for hours and his parents and sister were gone. He couldn't lie, not to himself and not at this point in their arrangement—he was pretty happy to see that she was still here.

He stepped from his car and made his way up the curved sidewalk leading to the back door. The light from the kitchen spilled out onto the porch, but he stopped before he even hit the first step. With the back door open and only the screen closed, he could hear everything coming from inside, and what he heard had his heart taking a tumble.

The song filtering out into the night was a familiar one to him, but he'd never heard it from Violet. He smiled because she wasn't quite the best singer he'd heard, but she was singing with passion. He continued to smile as he mounted the porch steps, but he didn't want to scare her so he remained outside the screen door and joined in, belting out the tune right along with her.

She jumped and stopped rearranging the floral arrangement at the center of his island.

"Sorry." He opened the screen and eased it shut at his back. "I was trying not to scare you."

"By singing like a bullhorn?"

Dax scoffed. "Bullhorn? Have you heard yourself?"

Violet tipped her chin and went back to the arrangement that hadn't been there when he'd left earlier. The arrangement was more greenery and tiny white buds than anything. He really didn't know much about flowers or plants, but he appreciated her eye when it came to things like this.

"I'll have you know I have a lovely voice," she informed him. "My dad always told us girls how pretty we sing."

"Maybe he was listening to your sisters." Dax chuckled.

Violet's lips pursed and he knew without a doubt she had to hold back a laugh. Dax moved on into the kitchen, still ridiculously pleased she was here.

He couldn't ignore the similarities between his past and his present. Junie used to sing in the kitchen. In the rare times they were home to share a meal together, she would sing or hum, and at the time he'd taken it all for granted.

"What are you still doing here?" he asked. "Not that you weren't welcome. I was just gone for quite a while."

"Three hours and sixteen minutes. Give or take."

Okay. Clearly she'd been worried or she wouldn't have been keeping track of the time. Something else he hadn't realized he'd missed. A woman waiting up for him. He missed having that companionship and all the daily moments to share with someone.

"Everything okay?" she asked.

He decided to keep Oliver to himself and let the young boy have a little bit of pride. Besides, Dax had faith things would work out just the way they were meant to. All for the good.

"Everything is fine," he confirmed.

"You might want to text your parents and let them know. I convinced them this town has hardly any crime and that you'd be perfectly fine. That's the only way I could give them peace of mind."

There she went again. She'd stayed here, obviously worried, but sent them on with assurances that he'd be okay.

Dax pulled his cell from his pocket and sent a message to the family group making sure everyone knew he was fine. Then he set the cell on the counter and made his way to the other side to stand next to Violet.

"So you've been singing and making this arrangement for three hours and sixteen minutes?" he asked. "Give or take."

She tossed him a grin. "Actually, no. I did something else first because I had some nervous energy."

"You were worried."

Violet's eyes widened and she swatted his arm. "Of course I was. You got a call and tore out of here like there was some hostage situation. Then you were gone awhile... What was I supposed to think?"

While her playfulness was adorable, it didn't override the concern lacing her voice.

As she stared up at him, tears welled up in her eyes. But she smiled through them and asked, "So, you're okay?" That unexpected reaction startled him and Dax wasn't sure whether to comfort her or give her a moment to recover.

Coming home to this domestic setting reminded him of all he'd lost. Yet none of this was real and he had to remind himself of that or he'd get swept up in this false world he'd created.

Yet Dax couldn't ignore the urge to comfort her. "I'm okay," he said. He reached out and slid the pad of his thumb across her damp skin. When her eyes opened, he cupped the side of her face as those misty eyes stared up into his.

"I'm just relieved."

Her words came out on a breath that it seemed like she'd been holding for a bit. Had she been that worried?

"It's silly, I know," she went on, attempting another smile. "And I know our little town has always been safe, but you just never know. Then I kept thinking of when my brother-in-law passed and how Jenn must've felt losing him, then how you felt losing your wife, which only made me feel more ridiculous because you and I aren't... We aren't..."

No, they weren't. But her emotions were running deeper than he'd thought and now he had no idea what to do with that nugget of information.

"You don't have to say anything," she added. "I'm aware I sound like I'm too attached and we've never even said we're friends let alone—"

He kissed her.

Without thinking, without second-guessing.

Dax closed that minuscule gap between them and covered her lips with his own. Violet gasped, but the next second she melted into him. Her hands curled around his biceps as she returned the delicate kiss. He knew he shouldn't be doing this, but he hadn't been able to stop himself the moment he realized she had feelings. But now they'd both crossed the line—a line he'd pulled her over, just like he'd done with the fake relationship.

Dax eased back, dropping his hand from her cheek. When her lids fluttered open, her eyes were still damp, her lashes even darker with the moisture. But she stared back at him as if seeing him in a whole new light.

Yeah. He'd really crossed a whole different type of line this time. He hadn't meant to kiss her, but apologizing now would sound like he regretted it. He didn't regret it, but he did regret this strong stirring of feelings. He hadn't expected this and he wasn't ready. He just... He wasn't.

"Did you kiss me so I'd stop crying?" Her words came out on a whisper and settled between them. Dax smiled, shook his head and swallowed the lump of guilt in his throat. Not once had he thought of kissing another woman since June passed, let alone actually doing so. But now that he had, he'd be rolling around those thoughts of remorse in his mind. He didn't want to feel guilty, but how could he not? He'd enjoyed the kiss, brief as it was, and he didn't know if he should be sorry to June for kissing another woman or sorry to Violet for not being able to move beyond a fake romance because now that he realized how much his feelings for her had grown, he was downright terrified.

Dax took another step back to give them both some space. He rested his hand on the edge of the island and glanced down to her bare feet.

Bare feet in his kitchen. Another image and moment that made him wonder what would happen if he moved forward, but at the same time too terrified to trust his judgment right now.

He shifted his gaze from her adorably purple-polished toenails up to the flowers on his counter.

"Where did you get those?" he asked.

"I pulled over on the side of the road and picked them on my way back from the feedstore and the clinic."

Dax blinked. "You ran errands to stay busy?"

"Kind of." She pointed toward the wall that separated the kitchen from the dining room. "I grabbed some supplies."

There were two large bowls and a clear tote with what looked like dog food, toys and a few other items inside.

Dax jerked back to her. "You grabbed all that for me?"

"You needed everything and I needed to stay busy." She shrugged and moved around the island, opposite of where he stood, and went to the tote and lifted the lid. "You have all you need in here. Leash, collar, a couple of toys I know Colt loves."

She lifted a green ball. "Even you know this is his favorite."

Dax chuckled and nodded but didn't dare cross the room. The space between them was necessary as he still tried to gather his thoughts. Though he doubted he'd be able to for a while, and definitely not with Violet still in his home.

"Since you said you were picking him up tomorrow, I thought I'd get you all set up." She put the lid on the tote and sighed as she stood straight up. "I can get out of your way. I just… I guess I wanted to make sure you were alright and then I went a little overboard shopping."

"This doesn't seem like too many supplies to me," Dax told her.

Violet wrinkled her nose in the cutest way, and he straightened and crossed his arms so he didn't close the distance and reach for her.

"I put a dog bed in the living room," she admitted. "And I put another one up in your room. I'm sorry. I promise I didn't snoop or do anything. It's literally sitting right inside the door. At least, I assume the bare white room is yours and not the other."

Dax groaned. "Why does everyone hate on my white walls?"

"Well, you have a new dog bed in your bland room," she told him with a smile.

As long as she was smiling and not crying, she could call his room bland all she wanted. Her smile radiated in any room—he just hadn't realized how much until he'd seen her tears. He hoped to never be the one to cause her sadness ever again.

"I really do need to get going," she told him. "I still have to get a few things printed for the event and I need to play with my own dogs so they know I didn't just abandon them."

"You didn't have to stay, but I appreciate your concern. It's been a long time since someone other than my parents and Clara worried about me."

Violet tipped her head back and gave him that sweet smile, but that reflection of sadness lingering in her eyes only tightened the guilt around him. Was she silently asking for more from him? Or was she just as confused? He didn't know, but he couldn't be alone with her and all of this tension and unease balling up inside him.

"Thanks for all the supplies," he told her. "I'll be by sometime in the morning to get Colt."

Violet headed to the back door, where she slid into her dainty sandals, then pushed the screen open. Glancing back one more time, she met him with those striking green eyes that held way too many emotions for him to unpack and examine.

Then she was gone, leaving Dax with the arrangement on the counter, the dog supplies and the lingering floral note of her perfume. She'd been filling his head for over a week and now she was filling his house. He had no idea how to move on and push through this barrier of emotions without getting hurt or hurting her. He'd pulled her into this situation and he was pretty sure she had stronger feelings for him now.

The question was—how did he feel and what would he do about it?

Chapter Fifteen

"Abby, I'm going to give Colt a bath so he's good to go before Dax gets here."

Violet stepped into the doorway between the kennel and the lobby area of the shelter as Abby placed labels on individual folders for each dog that would be available for adoption at the event. Abby shoved away a mass of red curls and glanced up with a wide grin.

"Oh, the sheriff is coming in to see you?" She wiggled her brows.

Violet shook her head. "He's coming to pick up Colt. I just happen to be here."

Abby made a dramatic turn to the computer. "You happen to be here at nine in the morning when you're usually seeing patients at the clinic," she stated, then turned her attention back to Violet. "Correct?"

Vi shrugged. "Maybe."

So perhaps she did scoot a few of her appointments around. She never would have done so for an emergency case and she would drop everything, including seeing Dax, if a crisis happened with any animal needing treatment.

But since Dax had kissed her last night, she'd thought of little else. She wanted to know why he'd done that and if he had regrets—or if he had feelings for her. Had he also lain awake most of the night replaying that moment over and over in his mind? Her stomach knotted and her lips tingled at the memory.

How could she tell him she'd started falling for him? This had all happened so fast and with little warning. They needed to talk, but what did she say? *Hey, I know I'm supposed to be your fake girlfriend, but I'd like to be your real one if you're over grieving your late wife and ready to move on?*

There was no good outcome for what she wanted and the reality that waited for her at the end of this two-week period.

"Hopefully I'll be done by the time he gets here but you can send him back if not," Violet added.

"Will do," the shelter manager said.

Vi went back to the kennel area and made her way down the concrete walkway between the pens. She hoped Oliver would stop by sometime today. She wanted him to walk a few of the animals that hadn't had much exercise lately, and with this nice, sunny day, this would be a perfect opportunity.

The moment she reached Colt's pen, he started wiggling and wagging his tail. His mouth dropped as he panted and he always looked like he was smiling.

"This is the best day of your life," she told him as she slid her key into the lock. "You're going home, but first we need to get you nice and clean. You're going to be so happy with Dax and I already have all of your favorite things at your new place."

Colt came right up to her and nuzzled his big head against her thigh. Violet rubbed on his soft ear as she reached for the leash hanging on the block column between his kennel and the next. She slid the loop around his neck and led him toward the wash room. All the barking and excitement from the other dogs seemed to give an extra spring in Colt's step as if they all knew what was happening. Violet loved adoption day. There wasn't much more that made her heart happy.

As soon as she got Colt into the room and closed the door, she slid the leash off his head and hung it on the hook next to the counter. Colt loved water so the moment she turned on the faucet in the largest bathing unit, he started dancing around.

Violet laughed as the water filled up. She turned on some music and grabbed the hypoallergenic wash and some towels. She started singing along to one of her favorite songs and she didn't have to tell Colt twice to get into the tub. The stainless steel basin sat low enough to the ground that he could jump over the ledge and into the water.

"You're such a good boy," she praised, as she rubbed the top of his head. "And you're going to smell even better when Dax gets here. You're going home to a nice big yard where you can chase all the balls your heart desires."

She pulled the hose down, spraying water all over Colt's thick fur, and couldn't help but smile at the visual of Dax and Colt having endless fetch sessions. That house and yard were made for dogs and children.

Had Dax and his wife wanted kids? Was that still something he wished for if he ever remarried? Dax would be a wonderful husband and father if that was something he chose to do. With his giving nature and servant's heart, not to mention the way he could make you feel special with just a smile…

She slid the hose back into place and uncapped the shampoo. She poured a hearty amount into her hand and lathered up Colt's coat. The suds quickly formed and slid between her fingers and she started with his head and neck. Colt gave her a kiss on the cheek with his cold, wet tongue.

"I know, buddy. I love you, too."

She continued to lather and wash while she sang. She wanted to do anything to keep her mind focused on work and not that toe-curling kiss.

Was Dax just able to turn his feelings on and off? Or perhaps he didn't have feelings for her at all. She wished she knew what he'd been thinking before, during and after that kiss. She knew exactly what she'd been thinking during that kiss. Nothing. How could she? The moment his lips touched hers all thoughts vanished.

How could a man be so right yet so wrong for her at the same time? Surely this was not the man God had chosen for her. Violet didn't even know anymore. She'd gotten used to the idea of being single and working and caring for her pets and she was just fine with that lifestyle.

Then her world collided with Dax—pun absolutely intended—and she'd been in a state of confusion since.

Violet turned the water back on and pulled the hose down once more to rinse the soap from Colt. But the moment she started spraying, he got excited and jumped up and out of the tub, sending suds and water everywhere. Violet didn't think to let go of the hose so she managed to spray herself and shoot the water across the room—directly into Dax's face.

Vi released the hose, which had it immediately retracting in place so at least it was just spraying into the basin now. Colt hopped and wagged his tail at the visitor and Violet couldn't stop laughing.

"I didn't hear you," she stated, swiping water from her face. "I promise I didn't mean to assault an officer of the law."

Dax chuckled as he removed his cowboy hat and hung it on a hook near the door. "No charges will be brought up, but I won't need another shower, that's for sure."

Colt continued dancing around Dax's legs, begging for attention. When Dax knelt down and started rubbing the dog's ears, Colt sat down, relishing the affection. Violet went to the cabinet for more towels and tossed one to Dax.

"I'm really sorry," she told him. "I didn't hear you come in."

He dabbed at his face with the towel. "Well, you were singing again."

"What's that supposed to mean?" she asked, wiping the water off her arms. "I happen to love that song."

"Your singing is growing on me." Dax patted his T-shirt and jeans and ran the towel over his arms as well, then he squatted down to attempt to soak up the puddles on the floor. "Do you want to finish him and I'll try to get this cleaned up?"

"I didn't know you'd be this early or I would've been here sooner," she explained. "I wanted to make sure he was nice and clean when he went home."

"I appreciate that." Dax set the soaked towel on top of the washing machine and reached for another. "I might have to call for reinforcements any time he needs a bath. I hadn't thought that far ahead about doing those things on my own."

Violet snapped her fingers to get Colt's attention. Once she got him back into the tub, she went back to rinsing the soap.

"You have nothing to worry about," she told Dax. "Colt loves water—almost as much as he loves playing fetch."

Violet finished rinsing the dog and then waited for him to shake himself dry. She wasn't disappointed and immediately got soaked once again.

"Well, that was fun. How often does this bath time have to occur?"

"All depends. If he's been out running or in the heat more, he will sweat quite a bit so you'll need to bathe him more often. Winter months could be cut down some."

Colt jumped from the tub and shook himself once more. Violet draped the towel over his back and rubbed over his fur to get out the excess moisture.

"About last night," he began.

Violet's hands stilled. No. This was not a discussion she wanted to have. She wanted to move on and pretend the kiss hadn't happened. Well, she wasn't that good at pretending because she couldn't stop thinking about it, but that didn't mean she wanted to talk about it. It was too risky. They'd strayed too far over the line last night and they needed to pull back before one of them got hurt.

"It's fine," Violet told him, concentrating on Colt. "We're adults, we kissed, we can just move on."

When he said nothing, Violet glanced up to see him standing close with his arms crossed over his chest. She couldn't tell if he was relieved that she'd given him an out or if he actually wanted to get into this conversation.

She took the towel and put it on the washer with the other pile, then went to grab the blow-dryer.

"It's important to get him brushed so his hair doesn't get all matted," she stated, keeping the topic on Colt. She reached to the top shelf for the brush she needed for his thick fur. "There's a brush in that tote I brought you."

"Vi."

She froze at the nickname he'd only used once before. Maybe he wasn't relieved she'd given him that out. He had that authoritative tone to his voice and there was no way she could side-step this any longer.

Fine. She was a big girl and was mature enough to hide her emotions and listen to whatever he had to say.

Violet pulled the brush down and turned to face Dax. "Yes?" she asked.

"I want you to understand that I haven't kissed a woman since my wife."

Violet hadn't even thought of that. She'd been too consumed with the actual act and how it made her feel; she hadn't put aside her selfish emotions and considered the inner turmoil he was facing.

He sighed. "First I convince you to deceive both of our families and then I give off mixed signals by kissing you."

"When you word it like that..." She shrugged, moving back to Colt. "I'm a big girl, Dax. I could have told you no when you asked and I could have stopped that kiss."

If she wanted to...

"I just want to make sure we're good," he added.

Good in what way? In a way that she wanted to see if there was more to this insanely bizarre connection they'd started? Or good in a way that they'd peaked at the plateau of friendship and there were no more steps to climb?

Without looking up, she focused on the dog and meticulous strokes of the brush. "We're good."

Because if she looked up, she couldn't guarantee what he'd see in her eyes or if the unshed tears that threatened to take over would spill out, giving her away.

Dax had no idea how he ended up at Four Sisters Ranch for a family dinner with both his family and Violet's family, but here he was right in the middle of the long farm table. Violet sat right next to him and on the other side was Rachel. There were so many conversations going on, he had no clue where to direct his attention, and the tension radiating off Violet made him want to rest his hand on her leg and reassure her everything would be alright.

But doing that would only be another one of those mixed signals he shouldn't give off. There was no way to console or comfort her without taking a step into dangerous territory. The last thing he wanted to do was play mind games or cause her more grief. The image of her standing in his kitchen, eyes welled-up with tears, was one he wouldn't forget anytime soon.

"Can I make an announcement while I have you all here?"

The chatter stopped at Rachel's request. Dax had never seen so many people gathered around one table for a meal like this. But between the town events and the ruse of this relationship, not only were Violet and Dax coming together more, their families were as well.

Dax hadn't counted on how well all of them would mesh together. His mom sat between Jenn and her adoptive daughter, Paisley. His father found himself in a sports conversation between Jack and Luke while Clara had gotten quite chummy with Erin and Jenn.

It was like every missing puzzle piece had been found and locked together.

So why was there still that unease in his chest?

"I've been keeping a secret for a while," Rachel started. "Jack found out months ago, but I wanted to keep this to myself until I was certain I could pull it off."

"What is it?" Sarah asked from one end of the table.

Dax shifted to see her a bit better, but leaned back so Violet could see as well.

"I just finished my last class to obtain my business degree with an emphasis in Agriculture." She beamed. "So I plan on starting my own business, trying to help other ranchers and farmers who are just getting started, and I want to help those in need who might be struggling."

The whole room seemed to erupt in cheers, but Will Spencer got up from the head of the table and came around and hugged his daughter from behind. He dropped a kiss on the top of her head and patted her shoulder.

"I'm so proud of you, honey," he told her. "You've been doing all of that while helping me at the ranch, running the event space and helping Jack with the feedstore."

"She's an amazing woman," Jack replied from the other side of the table. "I plan on making her take a week off and we're going on a delayed honeymoon."

"I can't take a whole week off," Rachel complained.

"You can and you are," her father declared as he made his way back to his seat. "You've earned it and we will get along just fine while you get a much-needed break."

Dax listened as everyone chimed in on how proud they were and how much Rachel deserved the vacation. Violet added her own praise, then went back to pushing the fried chicken and mashed potatoes around on her plate. With all the chaos around, Dax didn't think anyone else noticed, but he did. Something was off with

Violet. She wasn't her bubbly, bold self and he needed to do something to get her back on track.

But before he could excuse himself and ask her to join him outside, Jenn raised her voice over the group's many conversations.

"I'm beyond proud of you, Rach," Jenn stated with a wide smile. "I have an announcement of my own and I don't want to overshadow you. I was hoping maybe we could share this special day together."

"Of course," Rachel replied. "There's no over-shadowing. We can all have great news. We went through some dark times as a family, so let's all thank God for getting us through and celebrate. What's your news?"

"Luke and I are having a baby!"

The table once again exploded with excitement. Clara threw her arms around Paisley and hugged her tight.

"You're going to be the best big sister," Clara told her.

The little girl smiled up at Dax's sister. "It's been really hard keeping that secret." She giggled.

"I'm so happy for you guys. There's so much to be thankful for in our family." Violet came to her feet and eased her chair back. "If you'll excuse me, I'll be right back."

The room quieted as Violet made her way out, and everyone seemed to glance around like they weren't sure what to do or say next. Dax removed his napkin from his lap and placed it on the table.

"Excuse me," he murmured, pushing his chair back and making his way out of the dining room.

Maybe he should let Violet have her space, but at the same time, he'd gotten this ball rolling and the guilt and weight of what he'd done didn't sit well with him. He knew she must be stressed about the adopt-a-thon coming up, but he couldn't help but wonder if all of the joyous news moments ago hadn't added to Violet's heartache. Had his own mixed signals with the kiss played a part in her not seeming herself? She didn't seem to want to talk about it the other day, which was fine by him. He never wanted to hurt her—had never meant to hurt her.

He had to go check on her and make sure she was okay. But for the duration of their agreement, they'd be best to keep their distance. That way, they could get their personal lives back on track and avoid any more heartache.

Chapter Sixteen

Of course he'd follow. Couldn't a girl just have one emotional breakdown in private?

Violet didn't even care that tears streamed down her cheeks or that she kept walking until she made it to the barn behind the house. She wanted comfort and she'd always found that here as a little girl. Her farm and the livestock were always there, always that constant. When she'd faced stressful times in her past, she would come in here and pray.

And she was pretty stressed now.

Violet swiped at her damp cheeks as she stepped through the open barn door, but even the familiar smell of hay and horses didn't calm her nerves. She wished she wasn't so on edge, but with this farce looming over her like a black cloud, and her sisters doing exceptional things with their lives and moving forward, Violet had never felt this unsettled in her entire life.

The heavy bootsteps behind her echoed off the concrete floor. She didn't turn around. He'd seen her cry one too many times, and quite honestly, she'd cried more in the past two days than she had in the past year.

"You want to tell me what that was about?"

That low tone of his closed the distance between them and seemed to envelop her. She closed her eyes, wishing she could seek comfort with him, but how could she when he was the root of her emotional distress. Granted he'd promised nothing and she'd done all of this to herself, but she still couldn't keep putting herself in a situation where she sank deeper and deeper into Dax's world.

"I came out here to be alone."

"I'm aware and that's why I followed."

Violet sniffed as she reached the stall where Sunshine was housed. She reached up when her sister's horse came seeking attention. Violet slid her fingers down the velvety nose of the mare and attempted to control her breathing.

"That makes no sense," she told Dax as she stroked Sunshine.

Boots scuffed over the floor behind her, the sound growing louder as he moved in closer.

"When you want to be alone with your hurt is when you need someone the most," he explained.

"I'd rather you not see me cry, if you must know." That admission stung. "I didn't want to leave, but I couldn't stay in there because if I cried in there I would've ruined the moment. Stepping out was the only option."

Another tear escaped and Sunshine dropped her head and inched closer as if she could sense the pain.

"You didn't ruin anything," he assured her. "But I'm more concerned about you and not what's happening back there."

Of course he'd know the perfect thing to say, which only added to her guilt. She wished she could snap her fingers and be out of this situation, but that wasn't reality.

Violet dropped her hand and pulled her shoulders back. She blinked away the unshed tears before turning to face Dax.

But she hadn't expected that level of concern on his face. He'd left his hat in the house and his hair was all disheveled as if he'd raked his fingers through it on his march out here. His thick brows were drawn in, deepening the creases in his forehead. His stern jawline was set and his hands were propped on his hips as he stared directly at her. That unwavering gaze had her heart beating even faster, which only heightened her nerves.

"Listen, I appreciate you worrying about me," she started. "But I can't be around you right now. I'm a wreck and if I'm completely honest, this has all gotten to be more than I'd anticipated. Be-

tween our families loving each other and blend-
ing immediately, to the kiss and these feelings
I didn't want for you... My sisters have their
beautiful lives and I'm over here looking like
a fraud."

The words just came tumbling out and she
couldn't prevent them. She also wouldn't apologize for her feelings or who she was on the inside.

"You can't hold it together all of the time, Vi."

There he went with that nickname again.

"You're human," he went on, taking one step
closer.

"Yes, which is why I'm struggling with how
I feel for you," she admitted. "I told myself this
would be easy and the two weeks would fly by.
But we've still got a couple of days left and I
don't know how I got into this position of devel-
oping feelings for you. You never asked for this
and you never promised me anything."

"I loved getting to know you," he explained
in that softer tone of his. "And even our kiss
was special, but this is too much and too fast. I
just... I'm sorry."

Violet chewed on her bottom lip, trying to get
her quivering chin under control. "I don't want
you to be sorry. You're not responsible for how
I feel. But I can't lie anymore. Not to myself,
not to you and not to our families. We never

should've agreed to pretend we were in a relationship."

"What?"

Violet and Dax turned to the entrance of the barn where Jenn and Clara were standing. Dread filled Vi as she realized they'd overheard what she'd said.

"We didn't mean to eavesdrop," Clara stated quickly. "Jenn wanted to check on you and I was coming to get Dax out of the way because we could tell Violet was upset."

Wonderful. She hadn't wanted to ruin the day, yet here she was. She really needed to get her life back on track. Going against what was right often ended in trouble, which wasn't news to her, but she'd really thought she was doing this for the right reasons.

Violet started to step forward, but Dax held up his hand and stopped her.

"This mess is my fault," he started, facing Clara. "When you and Mom and Dad showed up worried about me, then the timing of Violet on my doorstep, it all just collided and I came up with a plan."

"A plan?" Jenn asked.

Clara and Jenn moved farther into the barn and Jenn's eyes met Violet's. Vi never wanted them to find out like this, but there was a part of her that was relieved they wouldn't have to keep pretending.

"Dax didn't want his family to worry," Violet explained. "And you and Rachel kept setting me up on blind dates that I don't have time for, nor do I want to go."

"So I thought we could pretend date for the two weeks my family was in town," Dax added.

"And fake break up once we leave?" Clara asked, folding her arms over her chest.

Dax nodded. "Like I said, I didn't want you guys worrying about me. I'm perfectly fine here and I just needed to give you peace of mind."

"By lying," Clara accused.

"Yes." Dax nodded. "We know this was wrong," he added. "But Violet and I are friends and plan to remain friends now that this is out in the open."

Vi inwardly cringed. She knew that was the original plan, but how could she just reverse her thoughts and slide them back to that time frame? That arrangement had been made before emotions got involved and before the kiss.

"I'm sorry, Jenn." Violet stepped around Dax and moved to her sister. "I'm so happy for you and Luke. I just needed a minute to myself. I didn't mean to ruin your exciting news."

Jenn wrapped her arms around Violet and pulled her in for a hug. "You didn't ruin anything and I know you're happy for us. But the rest of the family might not be so forgiving with this lie."

Violet eased back and sighed. "I know. I made a mess of things."

"Beyond the lie itself, our families really grew to love each other in a short time," Jenn went on.

"That doesn't mean we all can't still be close," Clara chimed in. "I wasn't fake dating anyone."

"We should probably go tell the rest of the family," Dax suggested.

Clara tapped Jenn's arm. "We can head back in and tell the rest of them they'll be in shortly."

Jenn kept her focus on Violet, but Vi smiled, hoping to reassure her sister that everything would be just fine. And it would… Eventually.

Once they were alone again, Dax shifted to face Violet. He stared down at her with those crisp blue eyes and she really had to steel herself against her attraction.

"At least we're done lying," he told her. "We can just do the friend route—"

"No."

The word just popped out before she could think, but now that it settled between them, she wasn't taking it back.

Dax blinked. "No?"

"I've pretended all I can. The lies stop now and that includes to myself."

Violet wanted to reach for him, to have him

hold her one last time, to draw strength from him, but she had to stand on her own now.

"I can't be around you and tell myself I'm just your buddy," she went on. "I'm your neighbor and Colt's vet if that's what you want, but that's where our relationship stops."

The muscle in Dax's square jaw clenched and she waited, holding her ground, but he said nothing. He merely nodded and turned, walking out of the barn and back toward the house. It wasn't until he was out of sight that she exhaled the breath she'd been holding because there was a sliver deep inside her that wanted him to tell her they could be more.

But his silence spoke volumes and Violet would be okay. She'd mended a broken heart once before and she could do it again. The problem—this was nothing like last time. These feelings went deeper than anything she'd ever known so she'd have to rely heavily on her family and prayer.

She had enough going on in her life; she'd just have to stay busy. But most of all, she'd have to make sure she didn't have any unnecessary run-ins with the sheriff because in order to move on, she'd have to avoid him as much as possible.

Colt was living his best life in the backyard playing fetch with Mike Adams. Dax laughed and waved as he made his way up the steps to the back porch.

The moment he stepped into his kitchen, he was immediately hit with the aroma of Italian. Garlic, tomatoes and pasta. His mom stood at the stove and glanced over her shoulder to offer a smile.

"Oh, good. You're on time. The lasagna is almost done and the bread just came out."

He looked around and another scent hit him.

"Where's Clara?" he asked.

His mom's lips twitched as she turned back to the stove and reached to press the button on the timer.

"Mom. I smell paint. Where's Clara?"

"She's around," his mom replied, busying herself with checking the contents in the oven.

Dax sighed as he headed toward the front of the house, following the strong paint fumes. The moment he turned from the hallway into the living room, he stopped in the wide arched doorway. It wasn't the pale yellow walls that had his attention, though.

Hands on his hips, he watched as she took the ugliest shark-shaped lamp from one end table to the other. When she put it down again and took a step back, she nodded as if pleased with herself.

"That's not staying," he told her.

Clara turned and laughed. "Of course it is.

This is my housewarming present because that last one for your old house broke. New house, new gift."

Dax moved into the room and glanced down to the most hideous metal base he'd ever seen on a lamp. "You outdid yourself. This is worse than the last one."

"Thank you." She beamed. "I wanted something unique and when I stopped at that antique shop in town and saw this, I knew I didn't need to look any further."

Dax simply stood there in disbelief. He'd have to hide this thing once she was gone and only bring it out when she came to town. No way could a shark lamp be on display. Granted nobody would be visiting him. Violet certainly wasn't coming over.

"I wanted to take your mind off everything that happened yesterday," she admitted.

"This is a distraction for sure," Dax admitted. But nothing would erase Violet from his mind. "Is that why Mom made Italian? Trying to distract from the paint fumes?"

Clara smirked. "I might have asked for that. But I promise this is the final project I'm doing. After all, we're leaving after Pets in the Park tomorrow."

Yeah. The big event that he wanted to dodge, but what would it look like if the town sheriff didn't even show up to one of the biggest events in Rosewood Valley? Not to mention this was such an important day for Violet, and despite how they'd left things, he couldn't just ignore this adopt-a-thon.

Her vulnerable expression of her feelings in the barn had left him unsettled. He hadn't expected her to open up and he certainly hadn't expected her feelings to grow. He couldn't lie to himself and ignore his own development toward her, but he also couldn't ignore the fear and worry of getting close to someone again.

"You guys don't need to stay," Dax told his sister. "Now that Violet and I aren't... Well, anything."

Clara tipped her head and turned to face him. "Just give her some time. She'll come around."

"Around to what?" Dax retorted. "I can't give more than a friendship."

"Can't or won't?"

Dax rested his hands on his hips, really wishing he wasn't getting into this conversation.

"Both," he answered honestly. "I can't emotionally invest myself at this point. Therefore, I won't."

Clara rolled her eyes. "Always so stubborn. You might have been faking this whole relationship thing, but I can tell you that you aren't that good of an actor. I saw how you looked at her, how you talked about her when she wasn't around. And the same with her. The two of you have a special connection and maybe it only came from this sham that bonded you guys together, but you can't deny it."

No, he couldn't. But that didn't mean he could just jump headfirst into something that terrified him.

"You can't live in the past."

"I'm not," he insisted. "I moved to start a new life, didn't I? That's what June would've wanted."

"And you think June would want you to ignore this second chance at love?"

Love? He'd never gone that far in his mind—had he?

"Dinner is ready," his mom called from the kitchen.

Dax raked a hand over the back of his neck and wondered what his sister had seen between him and Violet. How was she so certain that something was there?

The gnawing pit in his stomach ached, just the same as when Violet told him she didn't want him in her life anymore. He didn't want her completely removed, but at the same time, how did he take that leap when he wasn't even sure where he'd land?

Faith. That was all he needed. Just like when

he'd made this move and was unsure. He had to have faith. But for right now, he wanted to pray on this situation and figure out exactly what to do next because the last thing anyone needed was more grief.

Chapter Seventeen

The crowd seemed to be a new record for the Pets in the Park attendance, and Violet could only hope that meant more animals would be adopted than in previous years. Her whole family was in attendance, either helping out somewhere or walking around trying to steer people to the area with all the animals. Even Dax's family had come as they'd promised. She really wasn't sure if they'd feel too awkward to show up, but she should've known they were people of their word and willing to help a worthy cause.

She'd seen Dax come in wearing his signature hat, a T-shirt with the sheriff logo on the front, jeans and boots. He hadn't texted or spoken to her since the other night at her family's ranch. More than once she'd pulled up her phone to text and ask about Colt but stopped herself. Of course, it didn't help that the contact picture on her phone was that silly selfie he'd taken.

Why did he have to be so endearing? No matter how she thought of him, or how they'd left things, her heart still swelled with so much happiness when she saw that photo or thought of him.

A few days apart had done absolutely nothing to erase the short time he'd been deeply embedded into her world.

"Miss Violet."

Vi turned at her name and laughed when she saw Oliver with his face painted like a spotted leopard.

"I see you found the painting station." She chuckled.

"My foster parents just took in a little girl who's six," he explained. "She asked me to go with her and then she picked this out for me. I couldn't say no."

"That's very sweet," Violet told him.

He glanced down to his feet and Violet noticed his shoes were newer than last time she'd seen him. He was slowly allowing his foster family to embrace him and provide. Oliver was a strong-willed child, but Violet knew he had a bright future ahead of him if he stayed on the right path.

"Listen, I've been wanting to talk to you." He tipped his head toward a nearby bench under a tree a few yards away. "Can we go over there for a minute?"

"Of course."

She followed him to the area of the park with less event traffic.

"Is something wrong?" she asked once they'd gotten away from the noise.

"I'm sure Sheriff Adams has already told you but I wanted to apologize for the other night when I got into some trouble."

Confused, Violet started to ask what he was talking about, but Oliver kept going as if too nervous to stop.

"He told my foster parents that I'd be helping him with this new project and he wouldn't rat me out to them so long as I stayed doing the right thing," he went on. "But I figure you two are dating and he probably talked to you."

Violet crossed her arms and waited for him to continue. She'd heard nothing of this, but she certainly didn't want to interrupt. She had to assume this "trouble" might have been when Dax tore out of the house the other night.

"I just think he's not like other cops I've had to deal with," the boy went on. "I mean, I think he actually cares."

Violet's heart melted and she reached for Oliver. She held on to his arms and stared straight into his dark brown eyes.

"I assure you, he does care. So many people care about you and want to help you succeed."

"I just wanted to make sure you knew that

I want to keep volunteering at the shelter and taking your pictures when you need them," he quickly added. "I thought I should apologize for causing a problem and sneaking onto private property the other night. I promise I won't do anything like that again and I hope you won't ask me to leave the shelter."

She scoffed. "I wouldn't be able to take pictures half as good as you. You're not going anywhere. So don't worry about whatever happened the other night. Everyone deserves a second chance."

Oliver nodded, pulled in a breath and exhaled in a manner that Violet could only describe as relief. He thanked her, then turned and walked away, disappearing into the crowd. She had a really good feeling about him and wasn't a bit surprised that Dax had extended a kind gesture. She also wasn't surprised that he'd kept that incident to himself. He was an honorable man and she hated not having him in her life. For the past two days she'd been on autopilot trying to get every last-minute detail ready for the event, but now that it would all be over, with less to distract her, what would she do? She'd gotten used to texting or chatting with him. Not to mention she'd gotten close with his family.

Violet pushed aside her own struggles and made her way back to the festivities, noting improvements in this year's event as she went. She was the organizer and needed to focus. The cotton candy booth was clearly a hit and one she'd have to bring back next year. Face paint was as well, and from the looks of the line to the animal area, they were going to have quite a successful day.

She wished she could tell that to Dax.

As much as she wanted to pour herself into this adopt-a-thon and every guest here, she also wanted to talk to him. Two days had been too long and after speaking to Oliver, she'd realized something.

She surveyed the crowd, trying to find the black hat, but there were so many it was impossible to pinpoint the exact one she wanted.

When she spotted Clara chatting with Ben near the taco food truck, Violet decided to keep her mind on her own business and keep on moving. If those two formed a friendship or anything else, that was between them. But Violet did have to admit they looked adorable together.

Violet kept going and finally spotted Dax over on the stone bridge that crossed over the creek that ran through the center of the park. He was speaking with Garnet Trulane, and Vi hated to interrupt, so she took her time reaching them and hung back just a bit—but she was certainly close enough to hear more talk about Joe coming home soon.

"Well, I can't wait to meet him," Dax stated, flashing that signature smile that could charm any woman from two to ninety-two.

Then his eyes darted over Garnet's shoulder and he caught sight of Violet. She didn't look away and she didn't even pretend this wasn't uncomfortable, though that was precisely how she felt. An awkward unease coursed through her as he glanced back to Garnet.

"If you'll excuse me," he told the elderly woman.

Violet moved toward the edge of the bridge and Dax crossed over to meet her.

"I'm sorry," she told him. "I wasn't trying to interrupt."

"You didn't. Is something wrong?"

Everything.

"I just wanted to thank you for what you did for Oliver."

Dax adjusted his hat by the brim and shifted his stance. "What I did?"

"You know what you did the other night," she murmured. "He told me how you offered him an out and gave him another chance. Not every officer would show that level of kindness and I want you to know how much I appreciate it."

He nodded. "He's a good kid and knows right from wrong. We just have to make sure he stays with the right people who can show him the right way. I plan on inviting his family to church."

Heart of gold. The man wasn't perfect, but she was having a difficult time finding a flaw at the moment.

"He just told me his family took in another foster," Violet informed him. "A little girl this time."

"I'll make a point to stop by and see them to find out if they need anything." He pulled his cell from his pocket and typed in a note, then glanced back up to her. "Was there anything else?"

He seemed distant, but she couldn't have it both ways. She'd put that wedge between them when she said she didn't want anything more than a near business relationship.

"Actually, yes." She cleared her throat and tipped her chin. "I—"

"Violet."

She turned her attention toward the sound of her name and spotted Kay heading her way.

"Sorry to bother you," Kay said, then pointed toward the animal area. "There are some questions about two of the newest rescues and I'm not sure of the answers. I couldn't find it in their packets."

Violet didn't know if this was a sign from God preventing her from making a huge mistake, but she couldn't just ignore Kay's request.

"I'll take care of it," Violet assured her. "Thank you."

She gave Dax one more glance before excusing herself and forcing herself back to work, leaving him behind.

"I know, boy." Dax rubbed behind Colt's ears the moment he stepped in the door. "I missed you, too. Do you smell those other dogs on me?"

Colt was exactly the companion Dax needed and Violet had known they'd be the perfect match. He wished he knew what she'd wanted to tell him earlier on the bridge. The way she'd zeroed in on him right before his mother interrupted made Dax wonder if she wanted to discuss what had happened between them. But surely she wouldn't dive into something too personal in such a public place.

Dax took his hat off and hung it by the back door. When he turned back around, his eyes landed on that floral arrangement on the island. Violet had plucked each of those stems and blooms from the side of the road for him. How silly was it that he found that sentiment so adorable and sweet? Nobody had given him flowers before, let alone thought enough to pick them.

When she'd first come up to him at the park, it had taken all his willpower not to reach for her. He missed her with a fierceness he hadn't expected. But he wasn't ready for another big step. Hadn't moving to another state and taking a whole new position been a big enough stride for now? He needed to get good and settled before he could even consider the reality of dating or bringing a woman into his life.

Colt danced around near the back door and Dax opened up the screen to let his new best friend out. With the newly fenced yard, Dax was comfortable not going outside with the dog. He'd let Colt get some energy out while he changed his clothes. It had been a hot day in the park, and his family was still there helping with the event teardown, but Colt needed a break.

Or maybe Dax was the one who needed a break.

As Dax mounted the steps, his cell vibrated in his pocket. He stopped on the landing and pulled the phone out, feeling hope rise in his chest at the thought that it might be Violet texting him about what she hadn't had the chance to say earlier. But no. The message was from Ben telling him his parents were doing fine and he could return to work next week.

Dax sent a quick reply. He held his phone in his hand, with the overwhelming urge to reach out to Violet. He didn't like unanswered questions or the curiosity that would eat at him until he knew what she'd wanted to tell him.

He pulled her name up and stared at the screen wondering what he should even say. He'd rarely been at a loss for words. Wasn't his job to be a man of authority? Yet this one dainty woman had him afraid to send a simple text.

Phone still in hand, and not one word typed out, Dax moved down the hallway toward his room. He didn't like the chaos that seemed to be building inside of him. This unsettled portion of his life shouldn't be happening. He had a plan and everything was going according to how he intended until Violet Spencer had come into his life.

He hadn't expected her and he had no idea what to do next—but something told him the proverbial ball was in his court. True, she'd told him she didn't want to be his friend, but she'd also approached him with something on her heart.

Dax set the phone on his dresser as his attention landed on the wedding picture of June. The way she smiled at him had him smiling as well. He wasn't sad to see this beautiful face anymore. Seeing that image of her gave him hope that she would want him to be happy and step out on faith. June had always been a believer that everything happened for a reason and as difficult as it was to find that reason at times, he had to think that she would want him to reach out to

Violet. She'd want him to take hold of any happiness and joy that came his way and thank God for second chances.

He could practically hear her now asking him what he was afraid of, but the answer to that was staring him in the face. He was afraid of forgetting her or somehow replacing her. He was afraid of losing someone he cared about again. All of those ideas curled together around his heart and gave a viselike squeeze that left an ache in his chest he couldn't describe.

He grabbed his phone and went back downstairs. There were some things that a text couldn't convey. Dax might not have a clue what she needed to say, but he knew exactly what he wanted to tell her.

Violet had never been so exhausted or blessed as she was by the end of Pets in the Park. She didn't have the totals for the fundraiser portion of the event, but she did know that twenty-nine animals had been adopted and that families and singles had come from all over the state to find a furry friend. Thanks to her social media posts and all the people in Rosewood Valley sharing, the event kept growing from year to year.

She was so glad to be home and more than ready to crash.

Vi toed off her sneakers at the back door and

pulled her rubber band from her ponytail as the start of a headache threatened to overtake her. She wasn't sure if the ache was from her hair being pulled back all day or from her fake ex, whom she couldn't get off her mind.

She really should just tell Dax that she wanted to try to be his friend. If she couldn't have him in any other capacity, she would at least take that. Cutting him out completely seemed harsh and unnecessary. Maybe she'd get used to being settled into that friend box and her feelings for him would calm.

She doubted it, but not having him at all would hurt more than having him a little.

Violet wondered if she should text or call or just go over there. Would he even welcome what she had to say? After the way she'd treated him and cut off their friendship, she wouldn't blame him for telling her she'd had her chance. She'd known from the beginning that he was still grieving his wife—and hadn't he tried to tell her he hadn't kissed anyone since June, let alone tried dating for real?

Still, she'd never know if she had another shot if she didn't try.

Violet yawned as she reached for her shoes, but the doorbell rang. Of course, Stanley and Margot started losing their minds barking and running to the door. They'd yet to come to greet her but one unknown visitor and they were up and ready to defend.

Vi pulled her hair back up into a messy bun and headed toward the front of the house. The barking only grew more intense and she tried to console them, but they couldn't hear for all the noise.

"Guys," she shouted over the commotion. "We're fine. I doubt it's a serial killer ringing the doorbell."

She had to wedge herself between them to even get to the door, but when she opened it, she was surprised to see Dax's family on the porch.

"We just wanted to say goodbye in person." Kay's wide smile seemed sweet yet sad. "You were so busy cleaning up at the event, we didn't want to bother you."

"It wouldn't have been a bother at all," Violet assured them. "Come on in, but mind the attack dogs."

Clara bent down to show affection to both animals, who were too busy wagging their tails and sniffing the guests to be worried for their safety.

"We've got the car all packed, so we can't stay long," Kay added.

"And we need to stop next door as well," Mike told her.

To say goodbye to Dax. She'd also said goodbye to Dax, but now she wanted a do-over.

Once they were inside, Violet tried to usher her dogs farther into the living room, but they seemed quite taken with Clara and didn't want to leave her side.

"Sorry," Violet said. "I don't get many visitors so they're happy to see other people."

"No worries." Clara laughed as she was nearly knocked over by Stanley. "This makes me want a dog even more, but my schedule is just too crazy."

Kay reached her hand out and placed it on Violet's shoulder. "Dear, I hope that just because you and my son didn't work out, that doesn't mean we can't stay in touch. We've had the best time here and have just fallen in love with this town and your family."

Vi nodded and pulled Kay in for a hug. "Of course we can stay in touch. I consider you all friends."

As Violet eased back, the doorbell rang again.

"Wow." She laughed as the dogs started their barking once again. "This is the most activity my doorbell has had in years."

Stanley and Margot followed her to the door, and the moment she opened it, her stomach clenched.

"What are you doing here?" she asked Dax.

"I believe you had something you wanted to tell me earlier."

He remained on her porch, holding her in place with those vibrant blue eyes.

Vi glanced over her shoulder and almost laughed at the three sets of eyes aimed in their direction.

"I saw their car out front," Dax told her. "But this is about us. What did you want to tell me?"

She really didn't want an audience for this, but he was here now and she wanted him to know.

"I didn't mean what I said the other day," she started. "When I said I couldn't be your friend. If that's all I can be to you, then that's what this relationship will have to look like because I don't want to lose you completely."

He shook his head slowly. "Friends won't work for me."

Her heart sank and she knew she'd blown it. Her harsh words the other day had come out of pain and she hadn't fully thought things through.

"I understand."

She gripped the doorknob in her hand, hoping she could get through this humiliating moment before she fell apart.

"No, you don't understand." Dax took a step forward. "Friends won't work for me because I want more than that. We have something here that neither of us wanted to admit, but it's too strong to ignore."

Violet heard a gasp from behind her and she

wasn't sure if it came from Clara or Kay, but that didn't matter right now. All that mattered was the man standing in front of her asking for a second chance at his very own second chance.

Once again the burn of unshed tears overwhelmed her, and Dax reached for her. Those strong hands framed her face as he tipped her gaze up to focus only on him.

"Are you good with this?" he asked. "Are we going to make a go of something more?"

Violet smiled and nodded. "That depends."

His brows drew in. "On what?"

"Did you ever eliminate those tickets?"

Dax laughed as he inched closer and murmured against her lips. "What tickets?"

The moment his lips covered hers, the audience behind her started clapping and Violet knew this time they were doing this relationship thing for real.

* * * * *

If you enjoyed
The Sheriff Next Door,
don't miss the other stories in
Julia Ruth's delightful
Four Sisters Ranch series!

Available now from Love Inspired.
And discover more at LoveInspired.com

Dear Reader,

Welcome back to Rosewood Valley! I hope you enjoyed Jenn's and Rachel's stories. In this story, Violet finds herself in a bit of a predicament when she's cornered into a fake relationship with the new sheriff in town. Oops!

Dax Adams is a widower and looking for a fresh start in this small Northern California town. What he doesn't expect are his parents and twin sister unexpectedly showing up on his doorstep, then assuming his new neighbor is his girlfriend. One misunderstanding rolls into another, and Violet and Dax find themselves in a two-week relationship to keep his concerned family from worrying so much about him running from the pain of losing his late wife. This "relationship" also helps Violet dodge all those blind dates her happily married sisters try sending her on.

Two weeks sounds easy and fast, but the two find they might have just enough in common to form a solid friendship—and maybe more. What started out as a misunderstanding suddenly turns into more than either of them bargained for.

I hope you enjoyed the third book in the Four Sisters Ranch series. I have loved watching these characters develop, and Violet and Dax were so fun to write. If you missed the first two books, you can start with Jenn's story in *A Cowgirl's Homecoming* and then Rachel's book in *The Cowboy's Inheritance*.

Happy reading!
Julia Ruth

Harlequin® Reader Service

Enjoyed your book?

Try the perfect subscription for Romance readers and get more great books like this delivered right to your door.

See why over 10+ million readers have tried Harlequin Reader Service.

Start with a Free Welcome Collection with free books and a gift—valued over $20.

Choose any series in print or ebook. See website for details and order today:

TryReaderService.com/subscriptions